"I learned a long time ago the wisest thing I can do is be on my own side."
Maya Angelou

Bianca

WHEN DID my descent into darkness begin? Was it the moment Rio's goons kidnapped me off the street? Was it the moment I fell in love with my kidnapper? Or was it more recent than that? Was it last night when Rio put a Glock 19 in my hand, and I used it on another human being?

It doesn't matter when it started. I'm already here, in the murky waters of Mafia madness, with death on my hands and vengeance boiling in my blood like acid.

Turns out I will consider anything to get my daughter back.

Even if it means I have to kill my mother.

Rio forced me to head up here to bed for at least a little rest after everyone cleared out post-gun battle, but it's impossible to find sleep. My baby girl is missing, most likely being held by a madwoman, and even if the madwoman is related to me by blood, there is no way in hell I can relax enough to sink into the oblivion of slumber.

Instead, I lie here in our marital bed, as rigid as a plank of wood, my heart doing weird stress palpitations and my jaw and neck muscles clenched so tightly I have a permanent headache. At some point Rio joins me in bed, and at least then I manage to unclench my body slightly as his warmth and proximity wrap around me and coax my muscles into releasing some of their tautness.

I still don't sleep.

Neither does he. Rio's breathing remains even and quiet, but every so often his fingers clutch at my flesh, and then he strokes me gently as if he didn't mean to grab me so hard and wants to soothe any hurt his convulsive grip may have caused.

He was shot last night but refused to take pain medication. Yes, it only turned out to be a graze, in the end, but I'm assuming he still must be in a lot of pain.

Somewhere just past dawn, Rio releases a muted sigh and then slides out of bed with a muffled grunt before heading into the bathroom. I roll from my side onto my back and listen to the sound of the shower.

I've wracked my brain trying to figure out what to do next, but maybe I don't need to plan any action other than to wait. Penn made it clear from her comments that "they" will be in touch with details about how I can get Emilia back.

"They" being Rossi or my mother, presumably.

So, instead of trying to figure out how to find them, I just need to wait for them to get in touch, and then Rio and I can rush in and retrieve our daughter. Alongside Danelli and the

To my readers—thank you. Without readers, this series would not have come to life, and I am grateful for each and every one of you.

RUTHLESS ENEMY

DARK ENEMIES SERIES BOOK 3

ZOE DELANEY

AUTHOR'S NOTE

This is a *dark* Mafia romantic suspense book, and as such, there will be triggers for some readers, including kidnapping, use of guns, death, and a morally gray hero and heroine. This book and series are suitable for readers 18+.

various members of the crew who support the Agosti organization.

Yeah, sure. It's going to go as smoothly as that.

On the plus side of this awful situation, everyone in Rio's
employ has shown themselves to be firmly in our corner. Our
daughter may only be six months old, but Emilia is the heir to
the Carlotti-Agosti empire, and as such, she may as well be
made of pure gold as far as they're concerned.

I know they will all do whatever it takes to bring her
home safely to Rio and me.

I release a sigh that mirrors the one Rio let out a short
time ago, then look again toward the closed bathroom door.
It's been several minutes, and the shower is still running,
which is unusual for Rio. He's such a busy man he doesn't
normally linger.

A sudden yearning fills me, to feel his arms around me, to
lose myself in his heat and his strength, and before I have a
chance to overanalyze my motives, I'm out of bed and across
the room.

I knock quietly, then enter without waiting for an answer.
He's leaning forward in the shower cubicle, both arms raised
with his palms flat on the tiled wall. His head is hanging
down, and the water cascades onto his back, making rivulets
down his muscled form and over the dressing covering his
ribs.

The dressing must be waterproof. Either that, or he'll
change it when he gets out.

When I enter, his head comes up, and I meet his haunted
gaze through the steamy glass. He's hurting, and I suspect not
only physically. Rio is a man used to being in control, and
with our daughter gone, the control has shifted to someone
else.

He hates that, I'm sure.

He removes one hand from the wall and holds it out to me, and I know I've made the right decision coming in here. For both of us. I whip off the oversized T-shirt of Rio's that I chose to wear last night and slip into the generously proportioned cubicle alongside him.

His arms wrap tightly and pull me close, and I don't even have the chance to take a breath before his mouth crushes down on mine with a mix of need and barely restrained fury.

I open my lips and let him in, knowing the fury is not directed at me and welcoming his blistering passion in whatever form he wants to deliver it.

His fury matches mine. It is *my* birth mother—and my family's so-called "old friend" Rossi—who has ripped our lives apart.

While Rio has the might of his family organization behind him, guaranteeing an army whenever he needs it, I have nothing to call upon except myself and my still-fledgling connection to this man.

I mirror him in the frenzied kiss, biting at his lower lip and moaning deep down in my throat when his fingers slide into my loose hair and grip hard to tilt my head farther back.

His erection needs no coaxing. He is hard and ready from the moment he lowers his hands and drags my hips in close. The heat generated between us from his cock, evident even with the cascade of warm water coating our bodies, turns my belly to molten desire, and I break off the kiss and release a whimper.

"I need you." I breathe the words against his chest and then inhale his seductive male scent, enjoying the rumble that vibrates through him when I lift exploring fingers and flick at one of his nipples.

"No time for foreplay, little bird. Not today." His tone is rough, sounding like he's only just hanging on to control.

I know the feeling. It's the same for me.

"No. No time." My voice shakes so much I can barely speak.

He grabs me around the butt and lifts me up, my thighs resting on his powerful forearms, and I automatically wrap my legs around his hips before I remember.

"Wait! Your ribs!"

"I'm good. The pain is…necessary."

What does that mean? Then he smashes my back against the tiled wall of the shower, and my breath leaves me in a whoosh. My brain stops formulating questions. The action is more violent than I was expecting, but I don't care. The ache in my back mingles with the need clawing between my legs.

The hot water still flowing over both of us washes anything negative down the drain. Here, cocooned by steam and the scent of desire, the outside world disappears. I like it that way. I *need* it that way. A temporary reprieve from the horror waiting out there. Time for us both to just…succumb to instinct.

I need my husband to *fuck* me. And I need him now.

He lowers me until the head of his cock is seated at my entrance, and my whimpers turn to moans instead. I arch my back, rocking my hips and wriggling in his hold to try and push downward. I want his waiting flesh in me. Not teasing at my entrance. I want to wrap my vagina around him, suck him in deep, and let him fill my channel with everything he is.

I need to forget. I want us *both* to forget…

"You're fucking gorgeous, Bianca. *La mia bella moglie.*" His voice is hoarse, his eyes shining with strong emotion.

It isn't love, not in this moment, and yet conversely, I have never felt more loved.

We are powered in this coupling by rage and an intense need to obliterate the fear for our future.

I smile up at him, aware there is likely no humor in my expression. Only hunger. He understands. There is no answering humor in his features, either, even though his lips are also drawn wide in a semblance of a smile.

He is the only one to truly understand the terror that lies beneath my every half-panicked breath…

"Fuck me, Rio. Please. Make me forget."

Finally, he complies, shoving up and into me at the same time as he lowers me down. The action is hard and fast, and it hurts just a little. Too much. Too full. I gasp as his ready flesh leaves no room inside me for anything else except need. He fills me right to my core, deep, deep inside.

My body adjusts to the invasion, and pleasure spirals outward as I grip him with my internal muscles. *Want. Need. I will never let him go…*

"Oh, God, that feels so good, so right. Oh, *Rio*…"

"Bianca, little bird, I will never get enough of you." He thrusts so hard my whole body involuntarily jerks upward in his arms. "I can never. Get. Enough." He punctuates each of his words with a vicious thrust in which I sense all the pent-up fury he's been trying so hard to rein in.

"Yes." I meet each of his thrusts with urgent movements. "Fuck me hard."

I lose myself to sensation, writhing against him as he continues to pump hard into my body, over and over. Water gushes down from the shower head above us, the sound a sweet background for the moans and groans and gasps coming from both of us.

He lowers his head and takes one of my breasts in his mouth, suckling at the flesh before worrying the nipple with his teeth and tongue in an action that causes ripples to extend out from that sensitive point until it mingles with the ache in my core, and my whole body craves release.

I am so close to orgasm, teetering right on the edge. When he growls and nips hard at my breast, I can't hold in the barrage any longer. My insides begin to clench around his cock, and I become rigid in his arms before my body shatters in a violent climax that pulls a scream out of my throat as I ride him.

He follows me instantly over the edge, his roar muted against my breast as he jerks and shudders and releases deep inside me.

Eventually, the sensations begin to ebb, and he slips out of me and lowers me back to the cubicle floor. His fingers trace my belly, then up between my breasts to my neck, where he encircles my throat in a grip not punishing, but firm enough to hold me in place against the wall.

I keep my chin high, allowing his touch. No, *reveling* in his touch, as his thumb strokes gently up and down one side of my neck.

"You will have bruises, little bird," he murmurs, and I manage a tiny nod despite the prison of his hold.

"I know. I feel them forming already." My butt and thighs ache from where his fingers squeezed my flesh so hard. "And a bite mark, I think."

His gaze drops to my breast, and his lips twist slightly, as if he didn't realize until this moment what he did in the heat of his passion. "The flesh looks unbroken, but I will arrange for a salve anyway."

His hand drops away from my neck and he flicks my

nipple with the very tip of a finger. Even sated, the action causes me to shiver, as if my body would be up for more, should he choose it.

"I did not mean to hurt you, Bianca. Not today."

"I know." I wind my hands up over his chest and clasp them around the back of his neck, pulling him down so I can plant a gentle kiss on his still-twisted lips. "It's all right," I add when he draws back. "I needed the escape. You did, too."

I let go of his warmth before leaning over to flick off the taps. The sudden silence is cloying.

"What did you mean, the pain of this is necessary?" I stroke the waterproof covering over his gunshot wound, careful to only press lightly.

Though with what we just did, I suspect if it was going to pop open and start bleeding again, it would already have done so.

Rio's brows draw together. "It gives me motivation and sharpens my mind. A reminder that our enemy is dangerous, and one wrong move will result in injury or death. I underes-timated Rossi once. The pain helps me focus. I cannot allow him to best me again."

"That's it? It's not…"

How do I ask a man as powerful as Rio if he sees the pain as his due because he feels that he let his family down?

His eyes narrow, as if he can sense what I'm afraid to put into words. "That's it." His tone is dismissive.

He steps out of the shower, effectively ending the moment of intimacy, and reaches for a couple of large white towels from the stack on the countertop nearby. He hands one of them to me.

"We will get our daughter back, my beautiful wife," he says. "I promise you that."

Suddenly, I want to snap at him, to tell him not to promise something he may not be able to deliver. But what happened isn't his fault, and he doesn't deserve my misplaced rage. And out of everyone I know, he is by far the one best placed to ensure we do get our baby girl back, safe and unharmed, where she belongs. With us.

So, instead of ranting at him, or rushing over and pummeling him with my now-clenched fists, I nod quietly and bury my face in the fluffy towel, scrubbing hard at my eyes and trying not to imagine the worst.

Our daughter's maimed—or even worse, her tiny, *dead* body—flung onto the scrapheap known in this twisted crime-ridden world as *collateral damage.*

2

_____

"Revenge is an act of passion; vengeance of justice."
Samuel Johnson

Rio

MY ENEMY HAS SHOWN his face at last, and I will *destroy* him.

I stare out the window of my office on the ground floor of my riverside estate and concentrate on keeping my breathing slow and steady. I have to dispel some of this anger or it will affect my ability to focus.

A memory flashes into my mind as I study the once-again pristine grounds of the estate, where only last night the bloody battle took place.

My father stood over me as I lay on the mat of the boxing ring in his gym, Nicky in the corner looking bloodied but somehow triumphant. "You had the win, Gregorio. And then you lost focus, and your brother took advantage. You are a loser today, and you will always be a loser in life, unless you maintain control over that temper of yours. Rein in your anger, boy."

He held out a hand to pull me to my feet, and as soon as I was upright and steady, his ungloved fist came at me so fast I barely saw it. The blow knocked me straight back to the ground. I lost consciousness that time. When I came back to awareness, Nicky and my father were gone, and my mother's doctor was waving some kind of bottle under my nose.

Old-fashioned smelling salts, I found out later, but at the time, all he said was, "If you keep disappointing your father, he's going to kill you one day, young man. I can only do so much to keep putting you back together."

Losing control is not an option, I remind myself. I must keep the dark beast that lurks within me contained. Or Bianca and Emilia will suffer.

Self-doubt has crept in for the first time since I assumed the mantle as head of the family. It is neither welcome nor useful, and I push the recalcitrant thoughts and old memories down, imagining crushing them in my fist as thoroughly as I will crush Rossi when I find him.

I promised Bianca I would get Emilia back safely, and I intend to fulfill that promise.

Still, the inner voice continues to taunt me. *Will* we get her back? Clearly, I have misjudged Rossi for much of my life, and it has cost almost everything I hold dear.

What does it say about me—about my ability to run the Agosti empire, that I could have been so easily duped by another?

I begin to pace as I wait for Danelli to arrive, running through my actions and decisions so far.

There was no point moving us all to one of my other

properties, or one of my safe houses, or hiding out on my boat. They already came for us, and they took what is mine.

And I will kill every last fucking one of them for daring to go up against me and my precious family.

I turn from the window when I hear a voice outside my door, but not before I catch a glimpse of my reflection in the early morning-sun-touched glass. My lips are a thin line, and my eyes are pools of shadows in a paler-than-usual face.

Anyone who sees me right now will know not to challenge me in any way. Despite my resolve, my control is on a knife's edge.

It is barely half seven, but Dana is already at her desk in the anteroom. It was her voice I could hear—she has been working her way through the list of tasks I gave her when she arrived. Calling each of the family heads in the northeast region and filling them in on what occurred before issuing a request to attend a meeting here at the estate.

I suspect most already know—the jungle network is fast and effective, but I must at least put up a show of going through proper channels of communication. Just as the various heads will likely pretend ignorance and shock when they receive the call.

I buzz her and impart further instructions in a tone that leaves no room for error. I expect the majority of my crew to assemble here on the grounds. Fast. We need a skeleton crew to remain out at the various business operations that continue unabated, but the rest of the team needs to be here, finishing the clean-up of the grounds, reinforcing security, and readying to leave the moment we get notification of the enemy's location.

I need to know where that fucker Rossi is hiding, and I

expect results from our network of eyes and ears on the ground.

Finally, I stop pacing and take a seat behind the desk. I sip the double-strength coffee Dana delivered earlier, though I barely register the taste. It's almost cold, but I need the caffeine hit. My thoughts are scattered, and I must regroup. *Focus.* Once more become the ruthless family head everyone expects instead of a father afraid for the safety of his child.

The family heads—those who choose to accept my "invitation"—should arrive within the next two or three hours, and there is work to be done before then.

Danelli arrives a few minutes later. My second stands at attention, staring slightly past me over my left shoulder, as if he cannot bear to meet my eyes. His guilt and shame obviously ride him hard.

"Boss, whatever you need, I'm on it. I swear on my life."

He blames himself for last night's debacle. So do I. But luckily for Danelli in this moment, I blame myself more.

"Have every man you can gather ready to go on my order. We will move out the moment we have a location."

He nods stiffly. "Yes, Boss. They are ready. We won't fail you."

Again. The last word is unspoken, but it hovers in the air between us, tainting our relationship. Things will never be the same again between Danelli and me.

When this situation is resolved, he will no longer be my second. We both know that. I have no friends, only allies and enemies. Danelli has been a constant by my side for many years now, and I do not wish to think about what the future will look like without him. Nicky is next in line, and I already know he will relish the role. I am just not certain I will enjoy it quite as much.

"What do you have?" I bark out the question, more harshly than intended. "And look directly at me, damn it."

He sucks in a breath and releases it slowly before adjusting his gaze to meet mine at last. "We got confirmation from a couple different sources. At least six of the dead men are from Carlos Rossi's crew."

I nod, unsurprised. Still, it is good to have the fact confirmed. I grind my back teeth together. Rossi is a dead man walking.

And Rina will be equally dead when I find her, if it is true that she has aligned with my enemy. My mind acknowledges that thought and then scuttles away. I don't have time to deal with it right now. There are complexities around the action of killing Bianca's mother, of course. Consequences for my wife that likely will be far-reaching and long-term.

I tune back in to Danelli, who is still talking. "...and we got word from one of our men down at the docks about twenty minutes ago. A couple of the crew saw something suspicious at the wharf. A transfer from boat to car, from the sound of it. Someone caught the sound of a baby crying. Quickly muffled, but the moment they heard what had happened here, they reached out to let us know."

"A car?" I stretch my mouth into the semblance of a grin, but Danelli flinches slightly.

Clearly, no humor is on offer in my expression.

There are any number of unmonitored places along the coast they could have ducked into and switched out for another boat or a car. We'd have no hope of tracking them, in that case. Since they stopped at the wharf, though, Rossi and Rina may well have made a fatal error right there.

"They should have stuck to the water. Get a team onto

CCTV around the area and follow all possible routes out of—"

"On it, Boss." My second turns and takes a few steps away, pulling out his phone as he does so to make a call.

There are many who are quietly on my payroll, including those who have access to camera footage around the city. The Agosti reputation is far-reaching, and I will take full advantage of that in getting back my child.

When Danelli turns to me once again, his expression holds a faint hint of hope, where before, nothing existed but despair. "That means they are likely still local, or at least somewhere within the state. If they'd gotten away on the boat…"

He shakes his head, and I grunt. We are in agreement on that point.

I nod toward the door, intending to dismiss Danelli. "For now, we prepare for the arrival of the others. And we wait for intel."

His gaze sharpens. "Others?"

"Heads of family. I've had Dana sending out requests for the past hour. They will already be on their way here, if they know what's good for them. And if they are not, then that will show their hand, and they will be punished. They are either with the Agosti family or against us. There is no longer any neutral ground."

Danelli knows as well as I do that there never was any neutral ground. The Agosti empire is too large to have anyone other than allies. Or enemies.

Neutral does not exist in *La Cosa Nostra*.

My second's brows rise as he considers what I've said, and his lips part as if he has something he'd like to voice, but in the end, he simply nods. In the past, if he had an opinion

15

that differed from mine, he would have spoken up. Not today. Neither of us trusts what he has to say right now.

"They involved my family," I state quietly, but there's a thrum of emotion that lies beneath my words. I cannot fully hide my ever-present rage. "My *child*. They broke a golden rule when they did that. And if they got to *my* family, they could get to any of us. The others will come. I guarantee it. Either in person, or they will send a representative.

"Ready the conference room. And ensure that every one of our men is on standby. The moment we find out where they are, we hit them with everything we have. Understood?"

My second nods, his lips a thin line of determination. "Understood, Boss."

He turns to leave but pauses at the sound of a hesitant knock at the door.

"Come," I bark out, expecting Dana.

Surprise runs through me when the door opens, and it is Bianca, not Dana, standing on the threshold.

She's wearing a dark turtleneck sweater with black form-fitting pants and low-heeled boots, and even in the current dire circumstances, my lips unexpectedly quirk at the corners. I told her, out in the forest last night, that she needed to start wearing dark clothing in this line of work to hide the blood. Seems she has taken me at my word, perhaps not consciously, but the effect is almost mesmerizing.

She no longer looks like my elegant wife. Fragile, inno-cent, almost broken. Instead, she looks fierce and determined, and not a single inch of her conveys innocence.

Abruptly, my tiny flare of humor fades to nothing. She should never have had to concern herself with blood and death. As my wife, she should be protected from that side of life. Adorned with designer clothing and jewelry. Pampered and worry-free.

She shoots me a quizzical half smile, as if unsure of my reaction to her presence. "I'm sorry to bother you, Rio, but there was something Penn said before..." She wraps her arms across her middle but continues after only a miniscule pause. "Before she died. I know you were there, but you'd been shot, and maybe her words didn't fully register."

I vaguely recall the woman speaking, but Bianca is correct. The pain and blood loss did affect my ability to think clearly at that time.

"What was it she said?"

Her angst is almost palpable, even from across the room. I want to stride over and sweep her into my arms.

She takes a deep breath, and her demeanor changes. She drops her arms to her sides, and her fists clench. Then her chin comes up, and she meets my gaze with a flash of determination in her beautiful eyes.

Fragile little bird, or strong Mafia queen? She is both, my Bianca, and in this moment, I could not be prouder of my wife.

"She said they'd be in touch soon, and I'd be reunited with Emilia. I think they're planning to contact me, Rio. I'm guessing they don't know how..." She glances at Danelli, and color floods her pale cheeks.

He immediately takes a few steps toward the door around Bianca as if intending to give us privacy.

"Wait."

He stops abruptly at my order.

I suspect he should hear this, too. "Yes, Bianca? You may speak freely in front of my second."

Danelli straightens surreptitiously, as if my words have

given him the confidence to take ownership of his role once again.

She swallows hard, then says in a rush, "I don't think they know how I feel about you. My guess is they think I'm still being held against my will, and that if they contact me, I won't simply run to you with the information. I suspect they don't know that I've actually fallen in love with you. We could use that to our advantage by setting me up as bait."

3

"She was trying to walk away and hold on at the same time..."

r.h. Sin, *The Mind's Journal*

Bianca

IN THE END, it's far easier than I expect to admit the truth about my feelings for Rio, even with Danelli standing there listening in.

Because it *is* the truth. I *do* love Rio, desperately. He and Emilia now hold my heart, in a way that no one ever has before.

Rio and I may be dark and twisted in how we began, and perhaps even now, our dynamic is not what others would see as "conventional." In Emilia, though, we made a beautiful little ray of sunshine, and together, we are a family. I can't bear the thought of anything bad happening to either one of them.

My hope is that Rossi isn't yet aware of that fact, and if *he's* not, then Rina is unlikely to know it, either.

Rina. It's too hard to think of the woman as my mother. I *had* a mother. A loving woman who gave me a happy life, until the car accident that claimed her life and sent my father scurrying into the wilds of Thailand to try and escape his grief.

The sudden heat in Rio's expression at my words turns the warmth in my cheeks to a raging inferno, and when he holds out a hand, I run to him and bury myself in his embrace.

Eventually, I lift my head from the safety of his chest and speak. "The nanny said it would be soon, Rio. So, all we need to do is wait for them to contact me, and then you can use me as bait to go get Emilia back."

Rio immediately stiffens beneath my embrace, and then he grabs my upper arms and pushes me back several inches. His face when he stares down at mine is full of unexpected fury.

"I thought you were joking about that. My wife will not be *bait*. Not happening."

If it were for any other reason, I'd be twisting out of his arms and running for the door to escape the inherent threat in his expression, but this is our daughter we're talking about.

My jaw sets, and I narrow my eyes right back at him.

"For Emilia, I will do *anything*," I say firmly, and only faintly register a hiss of breath from Danelli over the rush of blood in my ears. "And if they contact me—no, *when* they contact me," I correct, "that will offer the best opportunity to find out where they are and get her back. They said I would be reunited with her soon, and that means either they intend to bring her to me, or take me to her."

Now I do twist out of his still-clutching grip, but instead of running, I lean forward and poke a finger against the firm muscles of his chest. "And when they do, you had better bloody well accept that and be ready, because if you're not, then…then…"

I falter at the shadows that shutter Rio's features. I'm pushing him too far. Even *I* know that. He folds his arms across his chest.

"And *then*, wife?" His voice is soft, dangerously so.

I can't back down now. Even if a rush of fear weakens my leg muscles and threatens to crumple me at his feet. "Then I won't tell you about it, and I'll go get her back on my own."

A little part of me is so afraid I feel like I'm about to pee my pants. I have poked the bear too hard, and he's awoken. *What was I thinking?*

You're thinking of Emilia, I remind myself as we stare at each other in a silent stand-off.

One beat passes, then another, and then the snick of the door closing behind me seems to break the deadlock. Rio glances over my shoulder, shakes his head, and snorts out a faint laugh that is as unexpected as it is a relief.

"You scared off my second. And that's no easy feat."

I glance behind and realize Danelli must have crept out while we were arguing.

"Understand this, Bianca. You are literally the only person in this world that I will ever allow to talk to me in that way. Anyone else, and you'd be dead. Or minus a finger or two. Danelli wouldn't be sneaking off like a coward. He would be in here arranging a clean-up."

I release a huge breath. How did I get out those earlier words when I could barely even breathe? I nod, taking a moment to allow my heartbeat to slow to somewhere back near normal range.

"I believe you," I answer softly when I finally feel less shaky. "And if you felt that was disrespectful, I apologize for my behavior. But I will never apologize for wanting to do everything in my power to get Emilia back, Rio. Never."

"Come here, little one." He folds me back into his embrace, and I sink against him without resistance, allowing his warmth to relax my tense body and enjoying his scent that permeates the air around us. His lips caress the top of my head, and then his voice murmurs above me. "I do not wish to put you in danger, my beautiful spitfire queen. But she is ours, and I see that you need to be involved in her return as much as me."

"Of course I do." I lean back and stare up at him. "It's my fucking *mother* who took her!"

As if either of us needs the reminder.

Just like that, the proverbial elephant in the room becomes real. We have to take down my birth mother in order to save my daughter. One will live, while the other…will not. I know Rio. He will not let any of his enemies live.

Nausea roils in my belly. Perhaps my horror at the impossible choice shows in my eyes because Rio's manner turns gentle as he takes my hand and leads me to the seating area in front of the fireplace.

He draws me down to sit beside him on the wide sofa. "You know I cannot let Rina live. If it is true that she is together with Rossi in this, then both of them must die. It is the only way to keep you and Emilia safe and the Agosti reputation intact."

Emotion wells up, strong and conflicting. I can't categorize what I'm feeling. The complexity of it is too hard to put into words. It feels like system overload—as if a whole roomful of people is shouting at me all at once, and I can't discern any particular voice from the crowd.

Rina *birthed* me. No matter what happened after that, she will always be my birth mother. Yet, it seems likely that she and Rossi are working together to steal my child from me. And that's so wrong on every level. She put her own grand-child in danger and tried to kill my husband as well as destroy his family business.

If she *is* involved, then I understand why Rio believes he has to kill her. In his world—no, I correct my thoughts, in *our* world—it is kill or be killed, which likely makes his next actions as inevitable as breathing. Rio must kill to protect what is his, because if he does not, then everything he cares about will be destroyed.

Rina and Rossi would have known that, too, the moment they decided to go up against Rio. They are as much a part of this world as any of us.

I stare down at my booted feet, my thoughts in chaos and the rush of blood in my head tunnelling my senses to almost nothing.

Kill or be killed. Is that the Mafia lesson for today? Or is it protect our own? Or family is everything?

What happens if your family is on both sides of the battle? How do you choose?

I'm not sure how much time passes before I register Rio speaking my name in an increasingly loud tone.

"Bianca. Little bird. Look at me."

I lift my head and meet his dark gaze, which holds both simmering anger and compassion. Is the compassion for me? Am I being that transparent?

He lifts a hand and offers a gentle caress around my

jawline. "I do not wish to hurt you with this knowledge. But you need to prepare for what is coming."

"Yes. I know what's coming. A war is coming. And this is the moment—even more than last night when I took that gun and shot someone to protect you—I have to choose my side."

I take a deep breath and let it out slowly, shakily, knowing I'm about to agree to something I never imagined I'd ever come around to. Not in a thousand lifetimes.

"I'm with you, Rio. You and Emilia are my family. My world. And I'll support you in whatever action needs to be taken to protect that world."

He opens his lips, about to answer me, but the cell phone tucked in my pocket begins to buzz.

4

"Motherhood. All love begins and ends there."
Robert Browning

Bianca

I STARE DOWN at the message on the screen, nervous tension sending a tremble into my fingers holding the phone.

Text back when you are alone.

Despite my bravado a few minutes ago regarding my determination to offer myself up as bait for Rio and his crew to charge in after me, I never actually thought about the reality of what that might mean.

This is real. Not a book, nor a movie. I'm about to put my life on the line, not to mention Emilia's. If I make one wrong move, everyone I love may end up dead.

For Emilia, though, I'll do anything, and I lift my chin and swallow before meeting Rio's intent gaze. "Right, then. Do I respond immediately? I... What do I do now? What should I say?"

Sudden sweat coats my armpits, and the phone slips a little in my grip as my palms become equally damp.

"Tell them you're alone in your suite."

I do as Rio instructs. Then I can't resist typing out a second message.

Everyone else is downstairs. Is my daughter okay?

Rio *tsks* but doesn't stop me from sending it. Two minutes pass, in which the only sound that permeates the silence in the room is the hiss of the gas fire nearby.

When my cell rings, I jump, and my heart immediately kicks into overdrive. I thought they'd text back, not call. The number shows as a private caller.

"Steady," Rio murmurs, his hand warm on my thigh, though I can hear the thrum of tension in his tone. "Answer it, and put it on speaker. Be very careful what you say, little bird. Do not spook them."

No kidding! I lift the handset and tap the green button, then switch on the speaker function. I don't need to pretend my anxiety and fear. It laces every word out of my mouth, every wobbly breath that passes my lips.

"Yes? Is this… Who is this?"

"Bianca, despite the circumstances, it is good to hear your voice once again."

Rossi.

Rio stiffens beside me, his features turning to stone as his lips press together.

"Carlos? Do you have Emilia? Is she all right? *Please…*"

"She is well, my dear. We have no intention of hurting her, I promise."

We? My breath hisses out on a tiny sob that isn't manu-factured. She's all right. For now, anyway. I hold on to that thought.

"What can I do? What do you need from me? I just want my little girl back. Please, Carlos—"

"Bianca." His tone changes slightly, cutting across my rambling with a new firmness. "We do not wish to hurt you, either. Far from it. I have someone here who would like a word. It will need to be quick."

A pause, and then a female voice comes onto the line. Her accent is strongly Italian, the sound a little husky as if the speaker is fighting emotion. "Bianca? Is that really you?"

Rio's hand on my thigh tightens in a convulsive fashion, and a tightness grips my chest.

Several beats pass before I'm able to answer. "R-Rina?"

I can't force out anything else. My throat suddenly hurts too much.

I didn't want it to be true.

Of course I wanted my birth mother to still be alive, but not this. Not her involvement with Rossi.

Tears well up and begin to fall down my cheeks, but I feel as if I'm frozen in place. I can't even lift a hand to wipe them away. It is a few seconds before I realize that Rio's hand is no longer on my thigh. His thumb caresses across first one cheek then the other, removing the wetness there. His gentle touch gives me the courage to go on.

"So, it's true, then? You... You're really...alive?"

I'm stating the obvious, I know, but my brain is like mush, trying to process. So many questions. So many things I could ask or say...or *scream* into the phone. But I don't. Instead, I wait for her response and bite my bottom lip so hard I taste blood.

"I am. And my granddaughter is with me, as she should be. She is safe, Bianca. I will never hurt Emilia. Her beautiful

27

little face… She is so much like you were at the same age. So perfect. I adore her, *mia figlia*."

Mia figlia? My daughter? I mouth the query at Rio, who gives me a short nod.

I return my focus to the cell in my palm, sudden anger pulsing through me with every heartbeat. *Don't you dare fucking call me that, you madwoman!*

"I want to be a family once again, my Bianca."

The specter of Francine rises up in my memory. And Leon. Even Penn, who was doing her best for Emilia in her own twisted way. All the people who have died in this battle already, or been injured, and for what? Because of this woman and her accomplice, Carlos Rossi, and a sick need to be a *family* once again?

The thoughts rattle round in my brain as if seeking release, but all I manage to let out is a strangled half laugh.

"I always wanted to find you, but I never knew where the nanny took you. I lost my husband that day, in the explosion, but I also lost my daughter."

Well, guess that answers at least one of my thousand questions. A little part of me wondered if, somehow, my birth father may be still alive, too.

"And now you are found," Rina continues, her voice full of emotion. She sounds as if she's holding back tears.

Like me.

"It is finally time. Ever since your *husband*"—she spits out the word, and my eyes widen at the sudden vitriol— "found you, Carlos has been helping me get things ready to reclaim the Carlotti name and fortune. It is ours, Bianca, not *his*, and soon we will be reunited. We have a plan to rescue you from his clutches, and then everything will be all right. It will finally be all right."

"Where are you? I'll come to you. Let me—"

The sound of sobbing cuts across my words, and then Rossi is back on the line. "We have spoken too long, Bianca, for today. We will come for you, soon, and when we do, you should be ready."

"I... Yes, I'll be ready. Please, I just want to be with my daughter. Don't—"

"Do not tell anyone about this call. If you do..."

His choice not to finish the sentence is somehow worse than stating his intent straight up. He'll what? Hurt Emilia? Kill her? Now that I've spoken with Rina, I can't imagine she would let that happen. But she sounds a little crazy, so who knows?

I swallow hard, knowing there is only one thing I can say. "I won't tell anyone. I promise."

"Swear to me. On your daughter's life."

Oh my God. I cross the fingers of my other hand and lie in the most confident tone I can manage. "I swear on my daughter's life I won't tell anyone about this call."

The reality is, I haven't actually told Rio about the call. I just allowed him to listen in. But it's a technicality. I know what Rossi was asking, and I've just sworn a lie on my daughter's life.

When the call ends abruptly, I close my eyes and send a silent prayer upward. *Please, God. I just kind of lied, I know, and I apologize for that. But please, please don't let them hurt my little girl.*

Don't let them hurt Rio, either. Please keep him safe, too.

Rio

29

DANA HAS CONFIRMED that every family—except the Rossis, of course—has sent a representative. The last of them have now arrived, and they are all waiting in the bunker conference room downstairs.

I take the time before heading in to pull Danelli aside in the corridor outside the bunker room to receive an update. The moment the phone call between Bianca and Rossi ended, I gave him strict orders regarding the coordinated response on Rossi's various properties. My second now confirms that my enemy's business and personal premises have been razed to the ground.

I did not expect my enemy to be at any of his known locations, and I am not surprised when Danelli confirms that fact. But at least now there is nothing for him to return to. It will take years to rebuild what my crew has destroyed in a couple of hours.

"I want a tracker on Bianca," I say to Danelli. "As soon as this next meeting ends. Fuck. I want multiple trackers on her. In her clothing, on her phone, on any vehicle she steps into. Do not let my wife move a muscle without knowing exactly where she is at any given moment."

"Yes, sir. On it. Although…" He hovers, clearly with more to say, and I wave my hand in an "out with it" gesture. "It might be better to try something less obvious instead. In case she's taken and searched."

"Go on."

"There's a new injectable-type tracker… Goes under the skin… We managed to procure several of them only a few weeks ago."

I tap my fingers on my chin, considering. "Is it safe?"

"I believe so, sir. It has been tested extensively by certain areas of government—"

"Then use it. Whatever it takes. If you fail to keep her safe, Danelli, you die. Is that clear?"

"Crystal, Boss. If I fail you again, I'll do it myself. You won't need to."

I turn away without further discussion. No need to say anymore. He is tasked with Bianca's life, and we both know the consequences of failure. His shame is still driving him, and his need to save face with my family and crew will be the best motivator possible.

I pause at the door of the conference room to allow the turbulence churning in my gut to settle. Whoever coined the term "gut-wrenching" knew what they were talking about.

On the other side of this door, they expect to see Rio Agosti, cold and logical head of one of the most powerful families in the country. Regardless of any internal weakness that this situation has exposed to me, the ruthless Boss is what I need to present to everyone else.

The bullied child who apparently still lives deep down inside me, alongside the black rage that grew from the bullying, must remain locked away forever from prying eyes.

The world must never know the true Rio Agosti. The boy who cried in his mother's arms when his father made him kill. There is too much riding on my shoulders to falter publicly in such a way.

The men in this room must never suspect even a hint of weakness, or I am a dead man walking. As are all the people who rely on me.

Bianca knows, a little inner voice reminds me. She has glimpsed the real Rio and somehow decided she loves me anyway.

As if my thoughts have conjured her up, a hand slips through the crook of my elbow. I glance down at Bianca standing beside me. I left her with her bodyguards almost two hours ago, and I didn't expect to see her here now.

"I'm going in there with you." Her voice is calm, her eyes resolute.

I rake my gaze over her attire. She is still in her kick-ass black. The sweater and pants are casual but sexy as hell, the way they cling so tightly and show off her slim form. Since our last meeting, she has swept up her hair into a high messy bun and added makeup that conveniently hides her pale features.

"No," I decide. "You need to steer clear of—"

"*Yes*, Rio. I *am* going in there with you."

Her mouth thins into a determined line, drawing my attention to the crimson lipstick with which she has lined her lips.

"We are in this together, Rio. I am coming in with you, but this time it will be as your partner and equal, not as someone pretty to adorn your arm and confirm your masculinity."

I blink, not sure if I'm more surprised by her words or her obstinacy. "I should bend you over my knee for that impertinence."

"Promises, promises." Her crimson lips lift slightly. "We can do that later if you like, when we have our little girl back."

Despite the smile, her eyes harden with a grimness I haven't seen in her before. The thought of conducting this meeting with Bianca by my side—especially in this mood of hers—is strangely exciting.

"All right. I will allow it."

She laughs lightly. "Will you now?"

I choose to ignore her little taunt, adding sternly, "Remember, the men in that room are piranhas. They will not respond as well to Emilia's kidnapping as they will to the perceived threat to their own various power bases. *That* is what I will appeal to in order to gain their support. Not our daughter."

I soften my tone. "Please do not ever think I'm not putting Emilia first."

"That makes sense, Rio. I understand. You do what you need to."

"Good." I pat the fingers gripping my forearm. "I do the talking. Is that clear?"

She grins again, a flash of humor gone as quickly as it appeared. "We'll see."

Then she pushes open the door, tugs on my elbow, and strides with confidence into a room full of the most dangerous people in the country, as if she doesn't have a single twinge of fear or anxiety in her body.

Only, I feel the sudden tremor in her fingertips. And in that moment, I realize my beautiful wife is as good at putting on a front as me. I have never been prouder of her, nor more terrified for her and Emilia's safety.

5

"Always do what you are afraid to do."
Ralph Waldo Emerson

Bianca

MY INSTINCT IS to turn and run. Back to my suite to sit in relative safety—or at least as much safety as is possible here now that the estate has been breached twice. Still, I would have Lee and Mitch on duty to protect me, and I could wait for Angel to return.

I would much rather do that than face all the latent power and not-so-latent cruelty staring at me as I make my way around the long conference table to where Rio's seat remains empty at the end.

But I can't run. Not this time. It is *my* child's fate they are here to discuss, and damned if I'm going to sit around upstairs while the men in this room decide the future on behalf of my family. I will not let that happen without my input.

The shift in my relationship with Rio is more evident right now than at any other time, even surpassing the beautiful moment when I gave birth to Emilia and he held our daughter in his arms.

He just let me get my way out there in the corridor. And his eyes flared with what looked like pride rather than annoyance when I flounced ahead of him in a most likely foolhardy way into this meeting.

I grip his arm more tightly than I intend, taking comfort from his warmth and strength. When we reach the head of the conference table, he gestures to one of the many security men dotted around the edge of the room to grab an extra chair and position it beside the one waiting for him.

"Gentlemen, I am stating the obvious, but my wife is joining our meeting." He waits until I'm seated before adding, "Any objections?"

He spears every man here with his hard, intent gaze, while in comparison I dart quick, nervous glances at the occupants around the table. Mafia bosses, one and all. Standing at attention behind them are a mix of security and men who look like lawyers, leaning against the wall with briefcases at their feet.

I have met most of these men once or twice socially, and of course they were all here at the previous meeting, with the exception of Gianni Martelli, who is staring at me now with his shadowed reptilian-like eyes and an unsmiling mouth.

I suppress a shiver, not wanting him to see that his scrutiny affects me in any way. Rio was correct when we visited Washington. I should not have antagonized the man at his daughter's engagement party. The people in this world have long memories, and they don't seem to forgive easily.

With another inner jolt that I hopefully keep from them

all, I realize Rio's brother Nicky is here too, seated next to Martelli. My brother-in-law scares the bejesus out of me. Not as much as Rio always has, but at least with Rio, I know now that he loves me. I suspect Nicky would crush me in a heartbeat if I ever hurt his family. His hardness is not softened by any form of love or affection for me.

The silence drags on. I am certain every one of them objects to my presence at the table. Women in this world are for decoration; they are not decision makers. It soon becomes clear that no one has the guts to speak up.

Bad luck, gents. You won't get your way today.

Nervous glances won't cut it in this crowd. I raise my chin and emulate my husband, staring down my nose at each of them and nodding politely at them all, one after the other. Martelli ducks his head so I can't read his expression. Nicky's lips quirk up in a wolfish grin.

Rio doesn't waste any more time in getting down to business.

"You are all aware of what happened here last night, so I won't rehash it. I now have confirmation that Carlos Rossi is at the heart of the recent attacks against our families. His intent was to destabilize us to the point that a turf war breaks out. While we are busy fighting and killing each other off, his plan was to stroll in and take over."

"With *her* miraculously recovered dead mother by his side." Of course it's Martelli who interjects with that gem.

"Yes, with my birth mother, Rina Carlotti, assisting him." I'm proud of the fact that my voice comes out sure and confident.

And I even manage to restrain from rolling my eyes.

Martelli grants me less than a second of his attention before turning to Rio. "Is that going to be problematic?"

I open my mouth to answer, but Rio shuts the line of conversation down with one harsh word. "No."

"What proof do you have?" Another man I saw last time they gathered here—I think his name is Sabino, from memory —pipes up. His tone is curious, not aggressive, and Rio dips his head toward the man.

"Rossi called my wife just over two hours ago and admitted his role in kidnapping our daughter. Bianca also spoke with Rina—" He holds up a hand as yet another man opens his mouth to speak. "And yes, the call was on speaker, so I can personally verify the woman is alive and very much a part of the proposed plot against us, alongside Rossi."

"He wants to destabilize all of us? Take over everyone's business?" I recall that man's name is Darov. He's been tapping his manicured fingers on the tabletop while the others speak. At Rio's nod, he adds, "Then it is a problem we all need to address. And quickly."

"Agreed," Rio says smoothly.

"So, what have you done already to contain this situation?" Martelli is clearly looking for weakness in Rio, hoping the answer will be nothing yet.

Ha, I think. *You don't know my husband.*

I may not have been privy to everything that's been happening behind the scenes this morning, but I've heard snippets of conversation here and there. I know Rio has many irons in the fire. His network is huge, and I'm confident he's on top of this as much as anyone could be.

Rio remains outwardly calm. I wonder if it's only me who can sense the almost-palpable annoyance that leaches from him every time Martelli opens his mouth. I reach across and touch his hand, which is resting on the table in front of him, and he slowly slides his fingers over mine.

If I can do nothing else for him in this moment, at least my touch may help to ground him a little.

"As soon as the clean-up here at the estate was completed, I arranged for teams on the ground at each of Rossi's known business and personal addresses. The moment the phone call ended, I gave the signal. All of the locations were hit"—he glances at his watch—"just over an hour ago. I didn't expect to find him in situ, and that proved correct, but I can confirm his business premises, and his personal estate and homes, have been destroyed."

"Destroyed?" Martelli raises a querying brow.

"Fire bombed."

I happen to be looking at Nicky, whose eyes widen before he purses his lips. He obviously wasn't privy to the plan. Then I become aware of shocked murmurs all around the table.

Rio doesn't give them a chance to process that announcement. He pushes on.

"We also have intel received from CCTV footage that has narrowed the man's current location to somewhere this side of Augusta."

I can't hide my tiny start. Surely, Rossi wouldn't be so stupid as to use the same place to house Rina and Emilia as he arranged for me all those months ago?

As if Rio is attuned to my every emotion, he shoots a glance my way and gives a miniscule shake of his head. Okay. So, not *that* apartment. But Rossi obviously has contacts in the Augusta area, and that's as good a place as any to start looking. For the first time since I realized Emilia was missing from the cot in her room, a flare of hope ignites in my chest.

"We are expecting another call to Bianca. Our enemies believe she is at my side against her will, and it is our belief they intend to collect her and take her to her daughter."

"She *was* here against her will." Nicky speaks softly, his eyes curious as his gaze darts between Rio and me. "Forgive me, but you are certain that is no longer the case, brother?"

Ah, the use of *brother* to remind Rio whose side he's on. Nicky is smooth, and clever, and clearly doesn't think much of me.

All good. I really don't like him very much at all.

I respond before Rio has a chance to do so. "I love Rio and our child more than anything in the world, *brother-in-law*," I say in as calm a tone as I can manage. "I saved your brother's life last night. Our enemies don't know that because the nanny is dead and couldn't tell them, but Rio knows. He was there, and conscious throughout. I had the opportunity to run last night, but I chose not to do that. And I never will. Not again."

A low murmur starts up again as the men begin to whisper amongst themselves.

Rio huffs out a small, annoyed-sounding breath. "I will do whatever it takes to bring down Rossi and Rina."

Somehow, even without raising his voice, he manages to speak over the top of everyone, and the murmuring stops instantly.

"My wife and I are united in our marriage, and we desire to protect what is ours. Now, it is decision time. Who is with me?"

He stares around the room, and a shiver runs down my spine at the sudden power emanating from my husband. He hides it a lot of the time and brings it out when it's needed.

This is the Rio everyone is afraid of. He's hovering right there near the surface; I can sense him.

I unobtrusively shrink down a little in my chair when he adds softly, "And who, gentlemen…is *not*?"

6

"The bond that links your true family is not one of blood, but of respect and joy in each other's life."
Richard Bach

Rio

IN THE END, every man in the conference room agrees to support me. Not that they have any real choice. But now the army amassing to march against Rossi is too big for him to fight against, and it is only a matter of time before we find and destroy him and every remaining member of his crew.

While we wait, I decide to move our base of operations back into the city and install Bianca in the penthouse apartment once again. With many of my men deployed in the recent attacks on Rossi's properties, the estate is proving too large and sprawling to adequately protect.

Until our enemy is destroyed, the mid-city building is a much easier proposition to guard. It is surrounded by other properties I own and monitored by a private CCTV system manned by my team. The building offers a more contained point of defense, and it will be far easier to detect if an attack is imminent from there.

Bianca makes no objection. In fact, her relief at leaving the estate is obvious, and in the limousine on our return to the city, she finally speaks up for the first time since we left the heads-of-family meeting.

"That place is haunted for me." She points behind us, back toward the estate gates disappearing in the distance. "Not just because Penn stole our child right out from under our noses, but because of the others who died there. Your aunt, Francine..."

"Yes. My aunt did not deserve what happened to her. But she will be avenged, Bianca, and soon."

"I know. I believe you." She looks down at the phone constantly clenched in her hand. "But I'm tired of waiting. How long do you think it'll be before they contact me again?"

"Hard to say. I am certain it will not be long, especially now that my crew has made their move on Rossi's properties. He will want to take what is mine in retaliation. And you, Bianca, are my prize. The one thing I value above all else. Everyone knows that by now."

"Thing?" She snorts a little, as if my words have offended her, but I mean no disrespect.

She *is* mine. And no one will take her away from me. Not even my archenemy and her crazy mother combined.

"There will be eyes on us, especially now," I add in warning. "Shall we give them a little performance when we arrive in the city?"

Her eyes narrow, and she studies me before nodding. She has caught on quickly. "They'll need to confirm if you're still controlling my every move? Sure."

42

The ride is over soon enough, even with the heavy traffic that hits once we reach the inner urban area, and I wait for my accompanying men to check our surroundings and signal their okay before I alight from the vehicle. Bianca stays seated inside, so I reach in and drag her out by her upper arm.

She staggers before righting and then releases a small sound of protest at the manhandling. She tries valiantly to pull out of my grip. I drag her into my arms and grind my pelvis against her belly. Even assuming there's most likely an audience, my cock has a mind of its own and instantly begins to harden against her softness.

"Behave, wife, or I will punish you. And I promise the punishment I mete out will be designed for my enjoyment only, not yours."

The tiny hitch of her breath is too low to be heard by anyone else. Then her head tips back, and her eyes flash with emotion as she glares up at me. She appears to be channelling all the pent-up rage over our current situation and directing it squarely at me.

Good girl.

Bianca has always worn all her emotions on her face, and whoever is watching will see that her anguish is genuine. Hopefully, they will attribute it as much to the hopelessness of being controlled by me as a natural concern for her child.

I slide my hand into her hair and grip the base of the messy bun that still secures her tresses. I give her head a shake for good measure. "Tonight, you will dress up for me, wife. And you will wear your hair loose the way I like it."

I bend my head and take her wide, delicious mouth with mine, devouring her sweet pliability with an aggressive kiss that brands her to anyone who may be watching as mine.

Mine.

It is all I can do not to groan aloud as I feel her resistance dip, and she begins to kiss me back. That won't do at all.

Abruptly, I release her lips and turn, dragging her through the building entrance. She sucks in ragged breaths and huddles into herself, and then suddenly she begins to sob.

When I push her ahead of me into the waiting elevator, my heart is pounding. Those sobs are real, not fake, and the sound tears my resolve to shreds.

I turn to the security guy waiting to punch the buttons and snarl at him. "Get out."

"But sir…"

"*Out!*"

He obediently jumps out of the elevator cabin, but credit to him for trying to do his job properly, he turns back to face me. "There are men already up at the penthouse. It's been swept, Boss. It's clean."

I give him a short nod and then punch the buttons to close the doors on his curious expression. When we're partway up, I hit the stop button and face Bianca, who is still sobbing, though much quieter now.

"Little bird, what is it?" I pull her into my arms, and this time, unlike outside, she comes willingly. "It's all right. You can calm down now. They won't have eyes inside the elevator."

"I know." She wipes her wet face against my shirt and presses against me as if needing the closeness. I'm not even sure she knows she's doing it. The action seems instinctive. "I'm sorry, I just…"

"Just what?" I prompt when she doesn't finish.

"I know you were pretending out there. It isn't that. It's just…everything. Worry about Emilia. Knowing I helped kill someone last night. That's awful, Rio. So awful. I haven't let myself focus on it properly yet. And then there's the shock over finding out my birth mother is alive."

She releases a small laugh, only the sound is hollow and sad rather than joyful. "And realizing she's not the kind of mom anyone would ever yearn for. It's the whole thing. I haven't had time to process any of it, not really. And I think it's just beginning to hit me."

I cup her chin and raise it until she has no choice but to meet my gaze. I want her to read the truth in my eyes. "You are strong, Bianca. You are my beautiful queen. And you will survive this. We both will. I will make sure of it."

Her eyes shimmer with more tears, but these remain unshed. "You can't promise that, Rio. Please don't say—"

"I can. There is nothing I will not do to have you and our daughter safe once again, Bianca. I give you my word."

She nods, then frowns a little. "*Why* do you love me, Rio? I don't really understand that. I'm not special. And…I don't know if you've ever given your heart to someone before. So, why me?"

Her question is like a gut punch. I struggle to consider how to answer it. Why indeed?

"I can confirm I have never been in love before meeting you. And as to why?" I raise my head and stare at my slightly warped reflection in the mirrored wall, looking inside for the truth.

"I don't quite know why," I admit at last. "There isn't any one specific thing, or a list of things, that I can cite. Why does any person fall in love with another? Because you're the person for me. You just are. And that makes you the most special person in the world in my eyes."

Her smile is wobbly, but genuine. "You're my person, Rio. I know who you are, in here." She taps my chest, just over my heart. "I've seen your darkness. I've seen *you*. I know some of the things you've done. Things you're likely to do again in the future. I don't like those things or those actions. Many of them are monstrous. But it makes no difference to how I feel, and it certainly doesn't stop me from loving you. Because you're *mine*."

"And you, little bird, are one hundred percent mine. Now and forever."

Unexpectedly, she laughs again, only this time there's a new note thrumming beneath it. "What was that thing you were saying outside? About punishing me if I don't...behave?"

I rear back and stare at her. "Bianca, I do not think this is the time to—"

"I need a distraction, Rio. Please." Desperation laces her tone.

I know exactly what she's doing, and it is not healthy. Shoving the dark things deep down inside, with the intention of dealing with them another day. Only, if she does that, the darkness will fester, and she will never heal from the trauma of the past twenty-four hours.

Personal experience has taught me that the darkness never stays contained if you ignore it. When we have our daughter back and our enemies are dead, I vow to get Bianca some therapy.

She jiggles a little in my arms. "We're alone in here, aren't we? They can't see us?"

I glance at the camera in the top corner of the cabin, and above her head, I mime a throat-cutting gesture then hold up five fingers. The tiny red light above the camera winks out a moment later.

"No one will be watching for at least the next five minutes."

"Five minutes? That's hardly long enough. I think, Rio, I have been a very naughty girl. And I want to know what you're going to do about that."

"I know of only one power, and that is the power of love."
Debasish Mridha

Bianca

PART of me feels so wrong asking for this now. But my thoughts and fears and uncertainties are chasing each other around in my head until I feel like I'm actually starting to go insane.

The only place I seem to find quiet and any kind of solace is when I'm in Rio's arms. I run my hands over his hard body, enjoying the feel of his silk shirt beneath my fingertips. I trace the edge of the bandage from his wound, not visible unless you know it's there, before exploring lower, dipping in between our pressed-together bodies to find and stroke the hard flesh between his legs.

The flesh that has already risen to showcase his need.

At least here, in the semi-private cocoon of the elevator

car, we have a few minutes to switch off from the outside world to explore each other's bodies. And attempt to forget.

He releases a low grunt at my touch and snags my wandering hand. "If you've been naughty, my wife, then you do not get to touch." He brings both of my wrists together and uses one of his hands to circle them, before lifting my arms above my head. Somehow, he twirls me around, and then forces me forward until my face and breasts are mushed up against the cabin wall. "I get to do *this* to you, naughty little bird."

The slap on my left butt cheek makes me jump, both from the unexpectedness and the sting. *Ouch.* He didn't hold back with that one. Sudden desire throbs between my legs as intensely as the pain of that smack. Just as the hurt begins to die away, he does it again, and then again, each smack on my ass ramping up the heat and the need.

All the while, he continues to hold my arms above my head, and even though I pull at his grip, trying to turn and face him, he is relentless. I can't move, pinned to the wall like this. I can't escape his spanking.

I whimper, overwhelmed by the sensation, and then my whimper turns into a moan when his hard cock grinds against my rear, forcing my mound into the cabin wall where I buck my hips and rut, eager for anything to ease the pressure in my clit.

"We have three and a half minutes left, wife. I am going to bend you over, and I am going to fuck you, fast and hard. You will come, but not before I tell you to. Understood?"

His voice is rough and hoarse. He barely sounds like the Rio I know. He is filled with as much need as me—I know him well enough now to know that.

The hand holding my wrists aloft releases me, and then

deft fingers make quick work of my pants. He yanks them down, almost to my knees.

"Bend."

A hand on the small of my back encourages me, and I bend forward and down, exposing myself to him.

Another smack, this one more intense than before as there is no fabric cushioning the blow, and then his fingers explore my exposed seam before dipping briefly into my channel.

"So wet," he mutters. "So ready."

I can't even answer. I have no breath for words.

Then the head of his organ nudges at my entrance, and thought disappears altogether. There is no foreplay. No need. I am so ready for Rio to be inside me. He slides in smoothly and then begins to pump, hard and fast just like he said he would, each thrust punctuated in between with a smack.

The feel of him filling me up, the heat and delicious agony of his spanking, coupled with his grunts and groans above me, pushes me to the brink of orgasm.

My clit is on fire, ready to explode, and all the muscles inside me tense up, primed and ready to shatter around him.

"I can't hold on." The words pour out of me in a groan. "Is it time…" *Oh my God. Is five minutes nearly up? I'm going to come…but he told me not to…* "Rio! I can't wait—"

"*Come*, wife!"

His command tips me over the edge, and I scream as I come around him, my legs turning to jelly. Only his strong hands on my hips hold me up as I lose myself to the ecstasy. Then he's there with me, coming too, his hot seed pouring into me and deepening my orgasm to something even greater.

"Oh my God." I hang limp, bent double and with Rio still impaled inside me.

Moments later, he whips out of me, pulls up my pants and

then his own, and then turns me around and drags me into his embrace. I wrap my arms around his waist, his heart against my cheek racing and his breath coming in uneven puffs.

Same as mine. Holy heck. Did that really just happen?

"Oh, my wife. You need to be a naughty girl more often."

I lift my head and stare up at the camera in the corner. Were they watching? A red light winks on, and I drop my gaze, snuggling back into Rio, relieved that our brief moment was truly just ours alone.

"Please take me upstairs, Rio." I don't want to leave the cocoon of this elevator, but life is waiting on the outside. "I think I may need a quick shower."

His laughter shakes my body a little, and he keeps hold of me while he leans over to push the button for the penthouse.

The car begins to ascend just as the phone in my pocket buzzes with an incoming text.

THE MESSAGE from Emilia's kidnappers is clear and the instructions simple to follow.

Tomorrow. 10 a.m. Saint Rita's Catholic Church in South Boston. Sit in the second to last pew on the right. Be alone, or you will not see your daughter again.

Saint Rita's? That's the church where I was dumped as a baby. I almost laugh at the irony. Things seem to be coming full circle. I was taken from Rina and Stefano and dropped at Saint Rita's all those years ago by my nanny, and now I need to head back there to try and get my own little girl back. From my birth mother.

Only I can't laugh because the terror of disobeying them about being alone fills me to the brim. I groan and wrap my arms around my middle as Rio takes the phone and reads the message in silence. In involving Rio, I am risking Emilia's safety. Perhaps her very life.

As soon as we reach the penthouse, he barks out instructions to one of the waiting goons, and a flurry of activity begins around us.

I hurry to my old suite, where I was kept when Rio first snatched me off the street. From there, I head into the bathroom, where I strip off and climb under a hot shower.

My hands won't stop shaking, and I drop the bottle of body wash twice before I manage to get some into my palm and lather up. Tomorrow. Make or break for seeing Emilia again. And possibly meeting my birth mother.

And then watching Rio kill her.

I have so many mixed emotions, but first and foremost, I know that I won't be able to let him do that. I understand his world now, at least a little, and his need to maintain dominance in a dog-eat-dog environment.

But not that. Not Rina. She can't be all bad, surely. She seems to want the best for my little girl, and that is the one fact I need to cling to right now.

I don't know how I'll stop him, but I'm going to have to figure out a way.

The rest of the evening passes in a haze of nervous tension. Only one thing stands out—the visit from a doctor who, accompanied by Rio looking on, gives me a once-over check in my bedroom before pulling out a syringe.

"Hell no." I glare at him, then at Rio, shaking my head. "No, Rio. I don't need anything to sleep. Or relax. Please—"

"Bianca, it is not medication."

"Oh. Well. What is it, then?" I eye the syringe with distaste.

This doctor has barely spoken, and he is looking at me as if I'm a specimen under a microscope. He gives me the creeps, and if it wasn't for my husband's presence, I would have ordered him to leave as soon as he arrived.

"It contains a GPS tracking device," Rio says.

I gape at him. His words don't compute. "A...what?"

"A microchip. Doctor Samuel will inject it beneath your skin, and it will enable us to track you, should we lose sight of you at the church."

My heart, already beating faster than usual, begins to race in earnest. "I'm not really comfortable with—"

"It is non-negotiable, Bianca. You wish to act as bait? I am allowing that, under sufferance, and because the idea makes a strange kind of sense. But I will not allow you to walk into danger without taking every opportunity to protect you." He steps forward and brushes my newly washed hair back off my shoulders. "I need to protect you, *mia cara*. This technology is not publicly available, not yet, but it is safe. We have access via certain channels, and it has been tested."

The doctor leans in, and I shrink back. What are the channels he's referring to? This sounds like government-related stuff. Do his tentacles reach into every aspect of life in this state? Hell, this country?

My thoughts are going haywire until I force myself to stop panicking with a shake of my head. He is my husband, and he is doing this because he wants to help Emilia and me to stay safe. Not kill us.

I swallow hard and sit up straighter from my position on the edge of the bed. "All right. Where do you propose to inject it?"

And will the damn thing hurt?

The doctor taps the back of his neck. "Move your hair."

Rio clears his throat, seemingly irritated with the medic judging by his sudden glare. "Doctor Samuel, I believe you mean, Mrs. Agosti, would you please move your hair?"

The doctor's eyes widen before he drops his gaze. "Yes, apologies, Mrs. Agosti, for my rudeness. Would you mind, please, moving your hair? I will inject the microchip at the back of your neck, at your hairline. It will sit subcutaneously, undetectable even if they're looking for something. You will barely feel a thing."

I shift my hair and turn my face away while he does his thing with the needle. There's a tiny prick and then an ache that lasts for several seconds before dissipating, and that's it. "How long will it last? And...will it move around in there?"

I have visions of a little piece of computer equipment floating around in my veins and getting lost. What if it blocks something vital and gives me a stroke?

The stress is likely to give me a stroke before this tiny microchip, I acknowledge wryly to myself. *Think of Emilia. I'm doing this for her.*

"It will sit just under your skin and will not move around. And when the purpose for it being there is complete, the chip can be quickly and easily removed under a local anaesthetic."

The doctor's work seems to be done. He packs up his bag and leaves the room, giving a strange little bow at the door, and I gingerly rub the back of my neck. I thought maybe there might be a lump, but it doesn't feel any different.

"Are you sure it works?" I ask.

Rio smiles gently. "Positive. This technology has been tested, and I have since read the reports. Now I feel much better, knowing I will have eyes on you, my little bird."

The reality of what the tracker offers begins to dawn. "This means I can go in on my own tomorrow to the church."

At his nod, I add, "Oh, thank God. I've been so afraid, Rio, that they'll sense I'm not alone. That they'll back out at the last minute, and we'll never get her back."

"We will, I promise."

As I step once again into Rio's strong embrace, for the first time, I allow a little bit of hope to enter my heart. Maybe we really will get our girl back safely, and somehow our enemies will just melt away into the dark shadows they emerged from and never bother us again.

Only, I know, as much as Rio does, that is never going to happen.

This is only the beginning, and an all-out war is about to break out on Agosti turf here in Boston.

And I still don't know which of us—if any—will survive.

8

*"Forget that prince. With your brain and your
resourcefulness, you can rescue yourself."*
Brad Meltzer

Bianca

THE HEAVY WOODEN door of Saint Rita's Church, only a
couple blocks away from the imposing South Boston Catholic
Academy, clangs shut behind me, shutting out the sounds of
the city and traffic and muting everything except my too-
rapid breathing.

I don't waste time glancing around. Instead, I slide
quickly into the wooden pew where they told me to sit. Only
then do I raise my gaze and study my surroundings.

I don't remember being dropped here, of course. I was
only six months old. Given what I know of my birth mother
so far, it was probably a good thing that this church's adop-
tion program took me in and found me such a loving home
with the couple I will always consider my parents.

If I'd been brought up by Rina, and possibly Carlos Rossi too... I shudder at the thought of how I might have turned out.

The inside of the church is quiet, the decor modest yet clean. There is a sense of peace and calm in the air, but that doesn't stop my pulse from continuing to skitter and my hands to shake as I grip the edge of my seat.

Where are they? Will they actually bring Emilia here? Can I trust them? Maybe it's all a ruse, and I'm about to die.

Okay. Calm down. Rio won't let me die.

I raise a hand and rub the back of my neck where the tracker is buried. I can't feel it there, but the knowledge of its presence helps to center my swirling thoughts and stop the panic from rising too high.

There are lit candles near the altar at the front of the space, and an older couple sits away from me, their heads bowed. A third person—a man in casual wear—sits near the altar. Beyond them, no one else seems to be here, but none of them are paying me any attention. They seem like genuine worshippers, here to pray to God for whatever solace they need.

I glance at the figure up on the cross behind the altar. Should I start praying, too?

Just as a hysterical laugh threatens to bubble up and out of me, and I'm about to throw myself down onto my knees, a man slides out of the shadows to my right and into the pew to sit beside me. His dark suit, serious expression, and those dead-looking eyes I'm starting to get used to in this world proclaim his profession. *Goon.* A Rossi goon, no doubt.

"My boss sends his regards." He looks straight ahead as he speaks, not at me.

"Carlos Rossi?"

He doesn't respond.

I clear my throat. "Please, where's my daughter?"

Finally, he turns to face me. "You are to accompany me. And if we see one hint of anyone following, you won't see your child again."

I swallow hard and look down at my hands. *Hell.* When did my fingers tangle up like that? I force them apart and smooth out the skirt of my dress before resting one hand on each thigh. I doubt I'm convincing either of us that my nerves are not just as jumbled as my fingers were.

"All right," I say. May as well get on with it. "Let's go."

He stands and slides out of the pew before slipping back into the shadows at one side of the space. I quickly follow, not wanting to lose sight of him. He leads me down a short hallway off the main worship area, and then we stop at a door that opens out into a side alley.

Another man is waiting in the alley, standing beside a large black town car and tapping his foot on the cobblestones.

The man from the church—in my head, he's already been dubbed Goon One—holds up a hand when I step outside. "We need to search you before we go any farther."

I nod, having been warned to expect something of the kind, and try not to grimace when Goon Two steps forward and pats me down. He is more thorough than I thought he'd be, and it's a little invasive, but at least his face remains impassive when his fingers dip under the hem of my dress and skim my inner thighs.

Finally, he takes the phone I was clutching in one hand, switches it off before removing the SIM card, and then hands it back to me.

"But—"

"You won't need that. There will be no more communication by phone from my boss."

"Okay." Thank God I'm clean—apart from the ticking time bomb beneath the skin on my neck, of course.

Rio told me before I left the apartment today what he would order his men to do in these circumstances, and so far, they've played it by the book.

When Goon One lifts my loose hair and pokes around in it, I hold my breath, but finally, he takes a step back.

"Nothing," he grunts to the other man. "Let's go."

Goon Two opens the back door of the waiting car, and they quickly bundle me in, then one climbs in beside me while the other heads around to the front passenger side and gets in beside the already-waiting driver.

Please, Rio, I pray, knowing how ironic it is for me to be praying to my Mafia boss husband instead of the deity I'm leaving behind in this church. *Please let this tracker in my neck work. Please keep Emilia and me safe.*

When we're underway, I try to mark our route from what I can see out the window. We're heading across the river and north, by the look of it. I see an I-95 sign and commit it to memory. Definitely north, at least at this point.

I must make some kind of inadvertent sound. I don't know exactly what alerts the goon beside me, but he grunts, then takes out a black piece of cloth from his suit pocket.

"Should have done this earlier."

Before I can say anything in response, he whips the cloth across my face, obscuring my vision, and fastens it behind my head.

"Wait! There's no need for—"

"Quiet. We have our instructions. Now sit still and behave, and we'll be there soon enough."

Nothing else to do but wait, and pray some more that things will work out in our favor. I just wish I could control my racing heart and calm the panic that keeps suggesting worst-case scenarios in my head.

Rio

IT NEARLY KILLED me to allow Bianca into that church without any obvious protection. Of course, I had three people waiting on the inside—within minutes of Bianca receiving the location, in fact. They waited all night, on the off chance that Rossi would turn up there with Emilia.

I didn't actually expect him to do that—I wouldn't, in his place. But it was still a possibility I had to consider, just in case.

The three on my team reported back that Bianca had been taken out a side door and hustled away in a black town car. They got a partial number plate as it turned the corner, and that partial is now being run through CCTV by staff on my payroll.

The embedded tracker is active. Headed north from what I've been told, which computes with our earlier intel about the area up near Augusta. Of course, there's a lot of land between here and Augusta, but Danelli is on it, and the team has been ordered to follow and be ready to attack, but remain at a distance.

We need to confirm our enemy's location and secure Bianca and Emilia, first and foremost. And then we go in, all guns literally blazing, and take those motherfuckers out.

Too bad my usual patience is non-existent when it comes

to my wife and child. This waiting game goes against everything I am, everything I stand for. My power hangs in the balance, and somehow it feels as if I've handed over responsibility to Bianca to save our family.

And that does not sit well on any level.

I will have to trust her as much as I love her. Even though trusting another human being with my very existence is something I've never done before in my life.

———

It feels like a long while since I've been here in my office above the club, but in truth, it was only a few days ago that we were supposed to meet here with Carnarvon when we got notification about what was happening at the estate.

The paperwork Carnarvon drew up regarding a trust fund for Emilia still sits on my desk, awaiting signatures from Bianca and myself.

I finger the papers, then pick up my phone and speak with Dana to arrange another meeting with my lawyer. Early next week, I tell her. When Bianca and my daughter are home and safe.

No sooner have I hung up than she calls straight back.

"Yes?"

"Gianni Martelli is on the line for you, sir."

I frown. What does he want? After the heads of family meeting at the estate, everyone quickly dispersed, and though lines of communication remain open, the usual channel for Martelli to approach me would be to go through my underboss—in this case, Nikolas, who has stepped up to the role with more vigor of late. Or even via Danelli.

It is unusual for Martelli to contact me directly.

I tap my fingers on the desk, gathering my thoughts. Trying to work out exactly what he wants that he couldn't say in front of the others. "Put him through."

Moments later, Martelli is on the line. I cut through his greeting, my patience stretched to the limit and my temper on the edge of explosion simply because I have no idea what is happening with Bianca right now. I do not wish to waste time talking to a man I despise.

"What is it?"

Martelli clears his throat, the only sign of discomfort, given his voice remains calm. "I have been thinking about our arrangement, my friend, and I have a new stipulation."

I narrow my eyes and swivel in my chair to stare out the nearby window. The sky is ominously dark today. Like my mood. "You agreed to provide men and weapons to support my family, Gianni."

"I did. And I will. But how would you like more? I can offer every man I have, if you agree to one key condition."

Every man? His power base in the Washington area is almost as big as mine. He is essentially offering to double my army. Why?

"It must be one hell of a condition."

"It is." He pauses, and this time, he allows some hesitation through in his tone. "What I am about to tell you must remain confidential, Rio."

"Agreed." He has piqued my curiosity, at least.

"My daughter, as you know, recently married."

"Last weekend, was it not?"

"It was. And I thank you for your generous gift for the bride and groom, even though you and your dear wife were unable to attend. But…the issue is…"

I resist the urge to bark, "*Out with it*," and breathe slowly, concentrating on remaining calm.

"The issue is, the groom was rather elderly, as you know, and he…"

"Was?"

"Yes. He…err… He died in their marital bed two nights ago, mid, well, you know. And my daughter is now without a husband. With the distinct possibility of her reputation being tarnished, should the exact circumstances of her husband's passing come to light."

I sit back in my chair and rub my chin. I was *not* expecting that.

"I am very sorry for your loss, and that of your daughter, Gianni. Particularly at this difficult time in our world with the threat of war hanging over us. But tell me. What does this have to do with me? And your *already pledged* support for our family in this Rossi situation? What condition are you expecting me to agree to?"

"Ah yes. Well, I understand your brother, Nikolas, is single. And eligible. Is he, by chance, in need of a compliant wife?"

I can't help it. My mouth drops open. He wants *Nicky*? For his daughter? I am glad I am alone in my office at this moment as he truly has thrown me.

When I am certain I have control of my voice, I say in as calm a manner as I can, "Yes. My brother is single, though I am not certain he is currently in the market for a wife. He enjoys playing the field, from what I am led to believe."

"Come now, Rio. You know how it works. He would not have to stop playing the field. And imagine the force of our conjoined families, should these beautiful young people wed and create children together."

I grunt. He's not wrong. To have an Agosti embedded in the Martelli family would be a huge boon for us. Though I never expected to be asked to arrange a marriage for my brother. For Angel, yes. That is expected for sisters and daughters. But for Nicky...

He will not take this news well; I am certain of it. *If* I choose to accept Martelli's offer.

"You are saying you will pledge every man in your crew in support of the Agosti family, should I agree to Nicky becoming your daughter's husband? Her *replacement* husband."

"Well, yes, but—"

"There is one thing I must know," I cut across him as he starts to stutter out a reply, "before I agree to anything. What *exactly* are the circumstances of your son-in-law's passing? Other than, presumably, in the middle of having sex. Was it a heart attack?"

There is a long pause.

"Sort of." Martelli coughs delicately. "His heart stopped...when my sweet Daniela put a knife through it."

The very last thing I expected from Martelli was an ability to make me laugh.

9

"There's a victory in letting go of your expectations."
Mike White

Bianca

I TRIED to keep track of time by counting in my head, but it was difficult to know if I was counting too fast, or too slow, or if I lost count altogether through sheer nervous tension.

I feel like we veered left at one point, and then right, but they could have been just bends in the road. Who knows?

I think it's less than two hours before the vehicle glides to a stop, but again, it's only a rough guess. Someone takes my arm and assists me from the car before hands fumble behind my head, and the blindfold is removed.

I blink in the sudden light, then stare around to find we're in a secluded estate not dissimilar to Rio's in size, from the look of the long, winding driveway. This property, however, appears less well-kept than Rio's, at least around the grounds and garden, which look a bit overgrown.

The house itself is a surprise when I turn to study it. For some reason, I was expecting the usual old-world grandeur that these Mafia bosses seem to love, but this place is the complete opposite. It's a sprawling single-story residence set against the hill and with floor-to-ceiling windows that must provide glorious views of the property along the whole front of the building.

If someone took the time to manicure the lawn and prune some of the trees and garden beds, this property would be truly stunning.

I gape up at the windows, looking for movement within, but quickly realize they're tinted, most likely to protect the privacy of those inside. No doubt they can easily see out. It would probably be a matter of security as well as aesthetics. I wonder if the glass is bulletproof as well as darkened.

I wrap my arms across my middle, then force myself to lower them back to my sides. Rio mentioned tells once. He said that action was one of my tells, letting him know I feel nervous, and I don't want to give anything away right now.

Is Rossi watching me from behind that glass? Is *she*? Rina? My heart lurches with a pang of adrenaline, knowing I may be about to meet my birth mother.

I still haven't fully processed the fact that she's alive, let alone that she kidnapped my child and has been plotting to try and bring down my husband and cause a gang war.

My feet don't seem to want to work. I stand frozen on the spot, until one of the goons pokes me in the back, forcing me forward.

Please let the tracker still be working.

We head up a short flight of stairs toward the wide, double-fronted entrance. The doors swing open just as I reach the top step.

My throat closes over, and despite my resolve to remain calm, sudden tears burn my eyes, blurring my vision. I blink them away, determined not to cry.

A woman stands there staring at me, her hands fluttering near her throat as if she is equally afflicted by tension.

Her hair is dark, neatly pulled back in a loose chignon-style bun. I note a few strands of gray around the temples, but other than that, there is no sign of age in her immaculately made-up face and straight-backed demeanor.

Is she really my mother? She's so very beautiful. I search her features for something—anything—familiar. Perhaps a hint in the shape of her jawline that matches what I see when I look in the mirror?

But her eyes…

Those eyes are not friendly. Not at all. They are studying me with a calculating air, and I only just suppress a shiver.

Remember, they think you're here because you want to escape Rio.

"Oh, *mia figlia*," the woman says, after a pause that stretches out just a little bit too long. "It is really you? Oh, *il mio cuore e pieno*."

The cascade of words snaps me fully out of the urge to cry.

I straighten my shoulders and take a small step toward her. "I only speak English, Rina. I don't know what you just said."

Her brows rise as if in hurt, and her wide mouth wobbles. But her eyes do not waver in their scrutiny. This woman is clearly good at masking her true self. I need to remember that.

"We will have to correct that, my daughter. I said my heart is now full."

"Where is Emilia? Is she…" Now it's my mouth that traitorously begins to wobble. *Fuck*. I need to stay calm and in control. No matter how crazy these circumstances are. "Is she okay?"

The woman nods and gestures for me to continue forward and step inside the building. "She is fine. Sleeping now. I will have her brought in for you shortly."

When I step past her, I awkwardly try not to touch her, but her scent wafts up and around me anyway. It is fresh and clean, nothing like what I expect. Though I didn't particularly have anything in mind. What does Eau de Murderous Kidnapper smell like, anyway?

I'm focusing on the small details because I cannot believe *I am actually here in the same room as my birth mother*!

She closes the door behind me and touches my arm, and then, despite my intention to keep a distance between us, she grabs me in for a full-body hug. It's too much. I gasp and try to lurch backward, out of her grip, but she simply holds me tighter.

Does Rina also work out, on top of everything else? No wonder Rossi loves her. She's beautiful, devious, and obviously physically strong, too.

Finally, she releases me and steps back, and I take a few deep breaths. When she gestures toward a doorway off to the side of the entrance area, I suddenly notice her left hand. It is scarred and disfigured, the flesh puckered and the skin shiny and pale.

She laughs lightly when she notices my stare. "It has been so long, child. It is an old reminder, but one I often forget these days. Come. Join us in the living area."

I can't help the question that pops out. "Did you get that trying to save my…your…Stefano?" I can't call a dead man I don't remember Dad, any more than I can call this woman Mom.

She simply shakes her head, so I shrug and precede her into a large, open-plan-style room that is bordered along the whole length with floor-to-ceiling windows that brighten the modern-looking space. That's all I notice before I see the man rising to his feet from the white leather sofa next to a huge stone-hearth fireplace.

"Carlos."

"Bianca. Welcome to our current home, my dear. It is so very good to see you again."

Rina breezes past me, taking my arm and drawing me with her over to the seating area. "Carlos, Bianca wants to know if I got my damaged hand from trying to save her father. Should I tell her?"

Rossi switches his attention to my mother, and the softening of his features is instantly noticeable.

Wow. He really does love her.

"It is up to you, my darling, how you wish to proceed here. Whatever you want, you should do. You know I will support you, always."

I stare between them, trying to figure out their dynamic. It is almost as if Rina is the one in charge, not Rossi. But then, he's always seemed a little obsequious, and look how that guess turned out. This little man, missing a finger thanks to Rio, almost bested us and stole our child out from under our noses.

Obsequious, he is not.

My character assessments seem to have been way off since the moment I was catapulted into this world.

Rina begins to laugh before pushing me down onto the

nearest sofa. There is something in the sound that sends a shiver down my spine. Something not quite right.

"Then I will tell her the truth," she says, after the laughter fizzles out to nothing. "It is time my daughter learned of her true heritage and took her place with me"—she shoots Rossi a glance before correcting herself—"with *us*, as we take control of the whole East Coast. And beyond."

Holy hell. It really is true. She wants to reclaim the Carlotti fortune. More than that, by the sound of it.

I stare at her, my eyes drinking in the details even as my brain is screaming that she must be crazy. At the very least, she sounds as power hungry as Rossi.

She has kept herself trim, and I felt the strength in her embrace just before. She's obviously physically fit, and there is barely a wrinkle marring her dark-eyed expression. My tummy does a strange little squiggle when I realize I do look somewhat like her.

This woman is Emilia's grandmother. Her only living grandparent, barring my adoptive dad, who is still somewhere in the back reaches of Asia.

If he ever returns home to Boston, I'll introduce him to his granddaughter, of course, but until then, the immersion in this world—Rio's, Rina's, and Rossi's—means that there is more for me here at present than anywhere else.

And if I'm being truly honest, part of me is hurt that my dad flittered off so readily, basically without looking back, and left me alone to deal with being kidnapped, forcibly married to a stranger, and then all of this on top...

I shut those thoughts down. They feel traitorous, particularly as my childhood and teen years were safe and happy. My mother—my adoptive mother—was a wonderful, loving soul, and in this moment of facing down Rina, the comparison is obvious.

I clasp my hands in my lap, trying to hold in my emotions. I miss my mom so much it hurts. I wish she were here right now.

Rina sits opposite me on the couch next to Rossi, who sinks back down immediately. He pats her knee gently as she leans forward and says in a conversational tone, "I did get this scar on my hand, dearest Bianca, in the explosion that killed your father. But not because I was trying to save him."

There is a sudden buzzing in my ears, and my face feels alternately hot and then cold.

I don't think I want to hear this. I don't want to know the truth. Not this. Not this.

She continues with a smile, seemingly oblivious to my mounting horror. "I had to make sure, you see. That he couldn't get out. I stood there, holding the door for as long as I could, while he burned and burned. It took so long, Bianca. So long. Finally, he died. And then, at last, I was free."

10

*"The scariest monsters are human beings and what we will
do to each other."*
Jared Harris

Bianca

"Y<small>OU MURDERED MY FA</small>... I mean, Stefano? Your husband?"
The admission is out there, and I'm unable to avoid it. The
announcement is so horrifying that something in me clamors
for clarification.

Maybe she didn't mean it the way it sounds.

Don't faint, I command myself. *Do. Not. Faint. Emilia is
here. Think of her. Get her in your arms, and then it will all
be okay.*

Rina's brow furrows slightly as she studies my reaction. I
wonder if my obvious shock has disappointed her? Was she
expecting me to be happy that she killed Stefano?

Even if I *were* here because I hate Rio and want to join

them in their mad quest for power, surely she should understand the magnitude of what she's just admitted to?

Rossi is studying me too, but his eyes are less puzzled than hers and more pitying. "Stefano was an evil man, Bianca. Yes, you have his blood, but you are nothing like him. He treated Rina for their whole marriage with the utmost disrespect."

"Oh!" I'm still struggling to draw in a full breath. At least now the sick feeling has receded a little, and I think I may be able to remain upright without bringing up my breakfast. "So, he was…abusive toward you, Rina?"

Can my family history get any worse?

She waves a hand about. "He was dreadful. Flaunted all his floozies in my face. Humiliated me, over and over and over…" She begins to rock back and forth a little, laughing again, and the dawning knowledge crystallizes into certainty.

It *can* get worse. It *is* worse.

My birth mother is bat-shit crazy.

Rossi rubs her back, patting her in a soothing fashion that looks well-practiced. Does he know she's insane? Surely he knows?

"Carlos helped me disappear for a while. Got me medical treatment for my burns. And when I was recovered enough, he sent someone for you, too, Bianca. Only, you had already disappeared, and we couldn't find you. We looked for years. But *he* found you first."

I remember Rio's pleasure at beating out others to find the Carlotti princess, as he called me in those early months. Now I understand who he was up against.

If she'd found me first, Rio would likely be dead, and I would never have found love—as strange and twisted as it is. I certainly would never have had my beautiful daughter.

"Where…" My voice comes out too high, and I try again. "Where is Emilia? May I please see my little girl?"

I find myself directing my words toward Rossi. Of the two of them, he seems the lesser evil right this minute.

"She's on her way. Rina sent for her—"

A knock at the door interrupts him, and at Rossi's terse, "Come," a young woman enters, holding a bundled-up infant in her arms.

I only just manage to stifle my instinctive shriek and jump to my feet, rushing over to the woman so fast I almost trip on the edge of the rug. The woman startles and attempts to lunge away from me, but I grab hold of Emilia and wrestle her free.

"She's *mine!*" I practically spit at her. "*My* daughter."

I turn my attention to Emilia, pulling at the blanket that swaddles her and checking her over as best I can without stripping her off completely. She looks well, staring up at me with a half-asleep expression. Thank goodness she seems unfazed by my frantic movements. I lift her up and squeeze her against me, pressing light kisses to her softly scented hair.

My daughter is okay. She's safe. And she's back in my arms where she should be.

Only now do I turn back to Rina and Rossi, still seated together on the couch and watching my reaction. Rossi looks suspicious, but Rina is smiling in an indulgent fashion.

"She is beautiful, *mia figlia*. A third generation of powerful Carlotti women primed to take over the world. Well done."

"I… Yes. She is beautiful. And one day she will be very powerful indeed."

That's the truth, and it doesn't seem disrespectful to Rio to admit that. But, judging by the scrutiny from Rossi, I need to start acting more like I want to be here.

If I don't, I suspect he will simply have me killed—most likely in an accident he can explain away to Rina, and then he and my birth mother will raise my little Emilia as their own.

A fierce longing for Rio comes over me as I stare down once again at my little girl. But he's not here, and if the tracker isn't working properly, he will have no idea where we are.

I reach out a finger and stroke Emilia's cheek, taking comfort from the softness beneath my fingertips. She turns into my touch before struggling to sit up in my embrace as she begins to wake up properly.

I perch back on the sofa and re-position her on my lap. I don't ever want to let her go again.

"She seems well," I say to Rina. "Have you been bottle feeding her? I was breastfeeding until…"

"Yes. She took to the bottle very well, according to her nanny."

I glance at the young woman, now standing off to the side and watching me from beneath lowered lashes. She doesn't like me; I can tell from her stiff stance.

I raise my chin. I am not giving her back. Not in a million fucking years.

It may have been the stress of the whole situation, but my milk dried up within a day or two of Emilia disappearing. I was so distressed I didn't even think to try expressing. When I realized the milk was gone, part of me thought it would just come back the moment I held her in my arms, but there's nothing, not even a twinge of let-down.

I got you to six months at my breast, little one. I whisper the words only in my mind, but one day I will say them out loud to her. *I wanted to do more for you. I'm sorry.*

"What happens now?" I ask, genuinely unsure of what

they have in mind and terrified it may involve separating me and Emilia again.

Rina smiles brightly as Rossi rises and lifts the poker to stir up the dying fire in the grate.

"Now, we show you to your room," she says, "and provide a light snack, given your long journey. Then, once you've had a chance to settle in, we will have an early dinner in the dining room."

"Okay. That sounds…nice." Will I be able to force anything past my lips without throwing up? I'll have to at least try.

I press another kiss to the top of Emilia's head, taking comfort from the fact that she's alive and unharmed. She smells both familiar and different. Her usual comforting baby scent is there, but it's overlaid with whatever soap or shampoo they've been using here.

How long before Rio finds us? I hope it's soon.

"I want Emilia in with me. In my bedroom. Please?"

Rina flicks her dark hair away from her face as she considers my request. "Yes, I believe that will be acceptable."

Rossi shifts beside her, clearly uncomfortable with the idea. "Do you not think keeping the child separate is a better—"

"I have decided. My daughter is the best person to look after my grandchild."

He shrugs but shoots me a look that confirms he's not in agreement with that strategy.

Why? I'm studying him, still trying to work out his motive in all of this. Surely, it can't simply be that he's a besotted male giving in to every whim of the woman he adores?

But Rina has moved on in her thoughts, and her next words chill me to the bone.

"After dinner," she says, "we will share our plans for bringing down the Agosti empire, killing your husband, and reinstating the Carlotti and Rossi families as the kings and queens we were always meant to be."

11

"We're our own dragons as well as our own heroes, and we have to rescue ourselves from ourselves."
Tom Robbins

Rio

"THEY'RE IN MAINE, Boss. Near Portland."

Danelli's voice at the other end of the line is almost vibrating with excitement, and for the first time since my daughter was taken, I admit to feeling a little of the same. I punch the button to place the call on speaker and then pace my office, back and forth. I can't sit still for this.

"You are certain?"

"We are. The tracker stopped moving over an hour ago, and we've pinpointed it to a property this side of Portland. Less than two hours from here, sir, even accounting for traffic. I've already got a crew on the way."

I take a breath and let it out slowly. I'm about to ask who owns the property, but my second anticipates the query.

"It's been rented out for the past two years, apparently, to a middle-aged woman who wanted privacy to nurse her ailing husband. The woman is registered as an Anna Dorano, but the Realtor identified a photo of Rina as her tenant. We had an old photo of her digitally adjusted to match what she may look like now. Not exact, but…we've got them, Boss."

"We have." I am so close I can almost taste the victory.

But Bianca and Emilia are still in the enemy's lair, and we need to get them out before any offensive is launched.

A knock at my door heralds the likely arrival of my brother. I summoned him to the city earlier, following my phone conversation with Martelli, but now that issue will have to wait.

"Enter."

It is indeed Nikolas who enters the room, and I wave at the phone to let him know I'm on a call.

"Danelli, Nicky's here. They have Bianca's location," I add for my brother's benefit.

He nods his relief and runs a hand through already messy hair, as if it's a gesture he uses regularly to release stress.

"First thing is to get my wife and child out of there safely. We already discussed this in general terms, but now that you've IDed the actual property, you have the intel you need?"

"Yes, the team is studying the plans as we speak. There are a couple of strategic entry points for getting into the house, and we can set up a diversion on the grounds. It's isolated enough not to cause too much of an issue. The nearest neighbor is miles away. We'll fine-tune the details shortly."

"You do not attack until my wife and daughter are out and safe. Clear?"

"Crystal, Boss. I will die before I let anything happen to them. I swear it on the Blood Oath."

The Blood Oath, known as *omerta* in some circles, is sacrosanct. His allegiance to my family is unquestioned. It is his recent failings, with the estate breached twice under his team's watch, that concern me.

"Send me the address and a rendezvous point to meet with you and the crew. I have additional men coming provided by the Martelli organization. They should be here in Boston before dusk, and I'll send them straight on up there." I shoot a glance at my brother, but now is not the time to disclose why Martelli is being extra helpful.

"Nicky and I will also be there for the kill. Danelli, do not move in without my say-so."

There is no way in hell I am letting anyone else take out Rossi, or Rina, for that matter. They are mine, and mine alone.

I end the call with Danelli, and Nicky's eyes light up at the prospect of action. I immediately pick up the phone again and arrange for one of my men to unlock the armory.

My brother and I are about to head into battle, and we will not go in empty-handed.

Bianca

WHEN I RETURN to my room after dinner, I place my now-sleeping daughter in her little cot bed and then race over to the door to check that the lock is engaged. I grab the chair that sits at a small writing desk near one of the windows and shove it beneath the door handle for good measure.

I need time out from these crazy people before I have to face them again.

All through dinner, I kept recalling that earlier conversation in the lounge area. Rina and Rossi sat opposite me during the three courses we were served, and Rina asked seemingly polite questions about my upbringing and my job at the animal rescue center. But I kept visualizing that poor man on fire in his car, trapped and terrified and no doubt in searing pain.

And she just stood there and let him die? Enduring her own scarring burns to ensure she got the job done. The father of her child!

I can imagine Rio putting a quick bullet in someone's head, which is dreadful in itself, of course, but to stand there and watch someone you're supposed to love burn to death, and be happy about it…

I'm learning that there are degrees of horrific in this Mafia world, and my husband is not at the top of the list.

No, that place belongs to my mother.

When the dinner remnants after dessert and coffee were cleared away, Rina leaned forward with her elbows on the dining table and talked a little more about her intention to kill Rio and every member of his family—barring me and Emilia—so that she and Rossi can step up and take over.

"We have someone working with us to make it happen. Though it is all much slower than I'd like. All these years, Bianca, I had no idea where you were. Rossi was looking for you on my behalf, and we knew Agosti was, too. I didn't want to make my move until we located you because it's all *for* you, my darling daughter. You and now Emilia, too. I want the Carlotti name back where it belongs. At the top."

For a moment, while staring across the dinner table into

Rina's eyes, I wish I were Bree Walker once again. Innocent and unknowing about any of this life. This messy, violent life.

But then the momentary wish fades away. I could call myself anything I want, but the truth is I'd still be Bianca Carlotti at my core. Carlotti blood runs in my veins. It always has, and it always will.

As it does for Emilia.

At least now, I am marginally more equipped to deal with the shit that comes with that legacy than I was when Rio first snatched me off the street.

I move my gaze to Rossi, who is watching me with a calculating air that disappears the second I lay eyes on him. Now that I know something of his truth, I can't believe I never saw through to his duplicitous nature.

Rina may want me here as her dear, long-lost daughter, but that clearly isn't Rossi's preferred option. I'm guessing he'd probably rather see me dead.

Still, it's obvious that he genuinely cares for Rina. In a twisted and toxic way. The fact that he's supported—and likely enabled—her all these years makes him as monstrous as her.

And she is a monster. I cannot hide from the truth about Rina.

Then something she's just said penetrates.

"You have someone working with you?" Does that mean they have someone on the inside? Someone in Rio's organization? My mind skitters through all the possibilities of who it might be, and I only just contain a shudder at the horror of knowing someone Rio trusts may well be working to bring him down.

I open my mouth to ask something else, but Rossi holds up a hand—the one with all his fingers intact.

"I think we should leave it there this evening, my dear," he says, directing his words to Rina. "Your daughter looks tired. She has been through a lot lately and probably wants to rest."

Rina peers at me doubtfully. "Tired? Oh, all right. Apologies, *mia figlia*. I should let you rest. We will discuss more in the morning."

And now, I'm holed up in my bedroom with the chair shoved under the door handle and wondering how I can get a message to Rio that someone he's currently working alongside may well be a traitor to his cause.

***

SOMETHING WAKES me from my already restless sleep. I'm not sure what it is. Perhaps it's simply anxiety? I check the time on the clock above the writing desk—2:15 a.m.—then slide out of bed to make sure Emilia is okay, but she's quiet in her cot. What was it that—

A half gasp hisses out of me, and I take a couple of involuntary steps back as a black-clad man rushes from the shadows of my en suite bathroom. The figure is across the room and has his hand over my mouth before I can make any more noise.

I breathe heavily behind his hand, both terrified and filled with hope. Is this a rescue, or something far more sinister? Then I register the voice speaking low in my ear.

"Bianca. Mrs. Agosti. It's me, Lee. We've come to get you and the baby out."

Lee? My bodyguard? I can't see his face as it's covered with a balaclava, but I recognize the voice and wrap my arms around his firm middle, hugging him tightly.

"You'll be quiet?" he asks.

I nod vigorously, and he slowly removes his hand from my mouth.

"Oh, thank God, Lee. Thank God. How did you get in? The place will be alarmed to the hilt."

I don't care how he got in, not really. As long as the alarm hasn't been set off. He's here, and that means Rio is close by.

"We have a top IT team as part of our crew. They disabled the system. It's only down for a few minutes, though, so we need to be quick. I'm going to do something you won't like, but I promise its effect is only temporary."

"What…"

He pulls a syringe from a pocket somewhere and turns to lean over the cot.

"Oh! No, don't—"

Emilia lets out a tiny squeak, and then she's quiet again.

"What have you done?" I hiss at him. "What did you give her?"

"A sedative. We need to keep her quiet for now. It was measured and prepared by a doctor based on her age and weight. She'll wake up fine in a few hours, I promise. No lasting ill effects, the doctor said."

I want to protest, but it's too late. I'll deal with that when we're out of here.

"Gather what you need, ma'am. You have"—he looks at his watch—"two and a half minutes max. We need to move fast."

"Turn away."

Lee instantly complies, and I quickly drag off the night-gown that had been left out for me on the bed and pull my own clothes back on. Then I race over to Emilia and wrap her tightly in one of the soft blankets from the cot before lifting her into my arms.

"Where?"

"Back through here." Lee indicates the bathroom door, and I start to follow but stop and grab Emilia's diaper bag from where it lay beneath the cot.

I checked it earlier and found it loaded up seemingly for a quick exit, with bottle, formula powder, diapers, wipes, and a change of baby clothing.

Bet they weren't thinking of *my* quick escape. More like their own, should they need to leave in a hurry.

Always be prepared. The motto fits perfectly for this crazy underworld life.

I rush after Lee, who is standing beneath the open window and positioning the chair from my dressing table beneath. The window is pretty high up, though, even with the chair.

At my sharp intake of breath, he says, "It's all right. Mitch is out there, ready to help. Stand up here on the chair and hand your daughter out first, then I'll boost you."

I know he's right. I can't fit through that window holding my baby. But it's still hard to make myself hand her out into the darkness to yet another shadowy figure.

"Mitch?" I whisper.

"Yes, ma'am," comes the thready voice. "Trust me. I'll keep her safe."

I reach out and hand her down, then throw the diaper bag out so it lands on the ground next to him. Moments later, Lee boosts me up until I'm balanced on my stomach halfway out the window. Another figure steps up outside, this one taller and broader than Mitch. Even in black fatigues, I recognize my husband.

"Rio."

His strong grip steadies me and draws me all the way out the window. I cling to him for a moment, shaking like a leaf. He really did come to rescue me. Me and Emilia.

"It's okay, *mia cara*. I have you. You will be safe soon."

This nightmare is almost over.

Then an explosion rips apart the night, and all hell breaks loose around us.

12

"You may have to fight a battle more than once to win it."
Margaret Thatcher

Rio

SCREAMS AND YELLS rend the air, followed by more explosions, and then the popping sound of gunshots breaks out from different directions.

I don't want to let Bianca go, but the diversion came a couple minutes too early, and now the building alarm is going off too.

The enemy has woken.

Leon launches out the window and lands in a heap on the ground before immediately jumping to his feet.

"Go." I thrust Bianca at him, then look at the other waiting bodyguard holding my daughter with a diaper bag slung over one shoulder. "Keep them both safe."

"On my life, sir," Leon says. "Always."

The other one—Mitch, I believe his name is—nods too.

Bianca's expression is slightly shell-shocked, but as Leon drags her across the grass toward the shadow of the nearby treeline, her voice floats out toward me.

"Stay safe, Rio."

Stay safe? I bare my teeth in a grimace, only just managing to contain my growl. My family and my organization will never be safe until Rossi and Rina are dead. It is time to do what I should have done years ago.

Put them down like the rabid dogs they are.

I pull my gun from its shoulder holster and head to the rear of the property, suspecting Rossi is likely to run from whichever exit point offers the lesser threat. Danelli and a swarm of my men, supported by Martelli's crew, are already at the front, and that's where Rossi will send the bulk of his own security.

I duck my head around the corner of the building and see what I half expected—a black vehicle that probably sports bulletproof glass is just pulling up near the rear entrance of the house. The back car door nearest the house swings open. Ready and waiting for the boss to flee.

There is only a short distance between the house and the waiting car—a matter of a few feet at most. Not much room for error. I smile grimly. Enough time for my enemy to take a bullet between the eyes. If I can keep control of my temper and not let my inner monster affect my vision or my aim.

I stay pressed against the wall, taking advantage of the shadows to prevent the driver and whoever else may be in that car from seeing me.

An unholy screech suddenly permeates the air. What the fuck is that?

Then I realize I'm listening to a woman having a temper tantrum. It's definitely not Bianca, who should by now be safely through the trees and almost at our bulletproof vehicle waiting on one of the side roads bordering this place.

Besides, she would never sound like this. So out of control and…animal-like.

My pulse quickens. Even though I now know it to be true that Rina escaped the explosion all those years ago, some little part of me doubted. No more. That must be Rina—who else could it be? She sounds insane.

Then I hear a man's voice, trying to soothe her. *Rossi*. Hatred burns hot in my blood, and it is all I can do not to rush the door.

Patience; I need patience. I am the predator, and they are my prey.

Remember that.

"Rina," Rossi says again, irritation now lacing his tone. "We need to leave, quickly. The men are holding the entrance, but it won't be long before they make their way here to the back. A minute or two at most, I'd say. Hurry."

"She's gone. They're gone. I'm going to—" The words degenerate once more into incoherent shrieking.

Judging by the volume, they must be just inside that door. I lift my gun and aim, holding it steady and waiting for my prey to come outside to me.

Moments later, a rotund male figure rushes out, flanked by two men whose presence block me from getting a clean shot. I squeeze in quick succession. One shot. Two. The bodyguards are down. Just as I squeeze another round, the shorter figure hunches down before launching at the car. I hit him, definitely, but it's not the kill shot to the head I was intending.

His side, maybe? The hip?

The car door slams shut, and the vehicle's wheels churn

up gravel as it takes off fast. So, he's decided not to wait for Rina Carlotti, after all.

Him or her? I have to make a split decision in that instant. I have no hope of catching that car on foot, so I decide to go after her. I speak into my ear mic to alert the team.

"Rossi's in the black vehicle heading up the driveway. Not sure if it's bulletproof, but I'm guessing yes. I shot him, but he's not dead. At least one more in the car with him—the driver. Carlotti woman's still in the house."

I leave them to it and turn toward the door of the house. Time to meet my mother-in-law in the flesh.

Bianca

"*GOD FUCKING DAMN IT*!" Lee's curse huffs out in the night air, cutting through the muted yelling and sounds of gunshots behind us.

Mitch is ahead of us with Emilia in his arms. I can see the car we're heading toward in the distance, and it looks like safety to me. Lee said it was bulletproof.

But a little part of me screams that I need to turn and go back to help Rio.

This is my birth mother, after all. My family mess that he's now tasked with cleaning up.

"What is it?" I ask when Lee doesn't say anything else.

We're carefully following the line of the long driveway but keeping off to the shadows and bushes as much as we can. The action is mostly behind us now, centered at the front of the house from the sounds of it.

Lee touches his ear again. He must be listening in to comms and not liking what he hears.

My heart skips a beat. "Is Rio all right?"

He glances my way, and his teeth gleam briefly as he grins at me. "Boss is okay. He shot Rossi, but the bastard's getting away."

The sound of a car engine enters my awareness, and instinctively, I know it's *him*. Rossi. The man who supported my mother in all her madness. The man who stole my child and wants my husband dead.

A rage I've never felt before rises up and almost chokes me. I stumble to a stop, shocked at the strength of my feelings, before turning to look for the approaching car. I can't see it yet, as we've come around a bend in the drive.

We'll never be free or safe while our enemy lives. The thought comes out of nowhere, and I forcibly shut off the little part of me deep down inside that still feels like Bree Walker. Or even Aria Lowe.

If I'm going to survive in this world, I need more than Bree or Aria can provide.

I straighten my spine. "Give me your gun, Lee."

"Hell no, Mrs. Agosti. Your husband would kill me."

"It's not a request, Lee. It's an order. I am Bianca Carlotti-Agosti, Rio's wife and partner, and I *order you* to give me your gun."

He still doesn't comply, so I step forward and simply slide the weapon out of its holster beneath his shoulder. Of course, he could have easily stopped me, but perhaps there's something in my eyes that confirms I am not playing around with this.

Not anymore.

I am a fucking *Mafia queen*, and it is time I stepped up and took control of my life.

No more kidnappings. No more fear.

After a second, Lee bends and retrieves a second gun from a holster at his ankle.

I raise the gun and falter for a second. It's different than the one Rio gave me. That one was a Glock, I remember him saying. I have no idea what this one is.

"How do I…"

He sighs. "Here. Safety on… Off, like that. Bullet into the chamber like this. Pull the trigger. It has kick, so be ready."

The approaching car is almost upon us. As it rounds the bend, I nod at Lee, then step out of the shadows into the path of the vehicle.

I don't stop to think. I simply raise my gun and shoot toward the vicinity of where I think the driver's head should be.

13

"In moments of pain, we seek revenge."
Ami Ayalon

Bianca

THE GUN JERKS in my hand, and the shot goes wide. Of course it does. I simply don't have the expertise for something like this.

But Lee doesn't miss. He fires a split second after me, and the windshield on the driver's side disintegrates. Then Lee drags me by the arm off the road and shoves me down onto the grass verge before covering me with his body. The car careens in the opposite direction of us and comes to an abrupt stop when it hits a tree.

The engine keeps revving, but that's the only sound I can hear other than Lee's harsh breaths in my ear before his raspy voice spits out, "Jesus, Mary, and Joseph. You're as crazy as your fucking husband."

The curse obviously is not meant as a compliment, but I

decide to take it that way. Slowly, when no return fire hits us, Lee slides off me and helps me to my feet.

The driver is slumped back in his seat, clearly dead. The top of his head is missing. His mouth is hanging open, and his eyes are black holes of nothing.

A crumpled airbag confirms that it deployed correctly, but Lee's shot killed him before the impact with the tree.

When the rear door of the car swings open, Lee shoves me behind him and raises his gun to aim at the man who staggers out of the vehicle.

Rossi. He's holding his side, groaning slightly, and even in the darkness, I see the blood that drips through his fingers as he presses his hand against the flesh above his hip. Lee said Rio shot him. That must be the bullet wound.

Slowly, he straightens, as much as he's able, and stares past Lee at me. "I knew you weren't with us," he says in a conversational tone. His breathing is labored, but he's still functioning enough to talk coherently. "I tried to tell Rina, but she wouldn't believe me. I wanted to have you killed, but she forbade it. You're only alive because she would never have forgiven me if I'd done what I should have the moment you first ran from Rio."

Wow. All that time, when I thought he was one of the nicer men from this world, he was harboring thoughts of murder.

"Was it you who helped her arrange Stefano's death? She couldn't have done that on her own."

I feel numb now that my earlier rage has dissipated. Too much to take in. I will deal with it all later—which seems to be my current catchcry. I am turning into a regular Scarlett O'Hara.

"Did you blow up their car?" I prompt when Rossi doesn't respond to my query.

He grimaces and slumps slightly to one side, as if his pain is becoming worse. Likely it is.

"I did," he answers slowly, after a pause. "And I would do it again in a heartbeat. Do you know how many women he flaunted in her face? How many times he raised his hand to her? She deserved better than that monster."

"So, you blew him up and then helped her escape and hide all these years. Why? I mean…*why*?"

Lee shifts impatiently beside me, but I need to know the truth.

Rossi tries to laugh, but it ends up a painful-sounding cough. "I could say for love, and it would be partly true. But love only gets you so far. Money, on the other hand, and power… I wanted Rina *and* the Carlotti fortune. But she was so obsessed with finding you…"

"And then Rio found me first." Thank God. I didn't know at the time how lucky I was that Fate brought me to my husband before anyone else.

"He did." Rossi laughs again, and this time manages a choked-sounding gurgle.

Maybe that bullet of Rio's got the lower part of his lung?

"But I had the last laugh," he adds, and there is true triumph in his tone. "I killed his parents when they discovered Rina was still alive, and the great Gregorio Agosti never knew it was me."

"You killed the head of the Agosti crime family? And his wife?" I shouldn't be capable of any more shock, but apparently, I am.

Blood is pounding in my ears as my heart rate riots.

Vaguely, I hear Lee muttering under his breath. Cursing again. He sounds as shocked as me.

"I did. So did Rina. We did that one together, in your name. So, you are complicit in their deaths, Bianca Carlotti-Agosti, even though you were only a child, and no one knew where you were. When Rio finds out that fun little fact, he will toss you aside like the trash you are."

He lifts his other hand, which has been out of view all this time, and before either Lee or I can react to the sight of his gun, there's a loud boom when Rossi pulls the trigger.

Lee goes down beside me with a surprised grunt, his gun dropping uselessly into the grass as he clutches his shoulder. And then he falls forward onto his face and lies still. Another Leon—lost to this goddamn awful situation.

I can't bear it. So much death. All because of my family. And me.

"Get in the car and drive, Bianca." Rossi staggers a little, but his gun remains steady. "Or die right here in the dark."

"No." Why are they killing all the Leons?

So much suffering. So much blood. It's everywhere, all around me, and I can't bear it...

"If you don't, I will hunt you down and make you watch while I tear your daughter into little pieces, then feed them to the sharks in the harbor. Get. In. The. Fucking. Car."

A squeal rises up my throat and bursts out of me. "You will *not* touch my daughter. *You* die, you motherfucking *bastard*!"

I close my eyes and pull the trigger, and then I begin to scream.

Rio

SCREAMING in the distance stops me in my tracks as I search for Rina room by room inside the house. Bianca? I would know her voice anywhere. What the fuck has happened for her to make a noise like that?

Blood leaves my face, and my heart almost stops as the screams intensify. *Emilia? Is our daughter...dead?*

I don't even think, just run. Back out the rear door and along the driveway, my legs pumping as hard and fast as I can, following the path the car would have taken...

More gunshots, but they're coming sporadically from what sounds like everywhere, so I can't tell if any are coming from the same direction as Bianca's screams.

Panic lends wings to my body until I round a bend to see Bianca with her eyes closed and arms outstretched, pointing a gun. There's a half smashed-up car beside a tree with a dead guy in it and two male bodies crumpled on the ground near her. My frantic dash slows to a walk, and I stop and scan the area, assessing for danger.

There doesn't seem to be anyone else nearby.

"Bianca." I call her name, loudly, trying to get her attention.

The screaming has died down now, but she's whimpering and wailing. Where's Emilia? What in fuck's name has gone down here?

I call her again, and then again, taking a couple steps closer each time, and finally she opens her eyes and turns her head to face me. The gun swings around with her, and I holster mine to avoid setting her off before closing the final bit of distance between us as slowly as I dare.

"Sweetheart. Little bird. It's me, Rio. Put the gun down,

97

mia cara. You do not want to shoot the wrong person, now, do you?"

She blinks a few times, as if just becoming aware of her surroundings, and drops the weapon with a gasp. I wince, grateful the gun didn't accidentally discharge and hit either of us.

As soon as she does that, I swoop in and take her into my arms. Her body is shaking, and sobs wrack her as she sinks into my embrace.

I stare over her head at the two downed men. Rossi. And her bodyguard. It's pretty obvious Rossi is dead. There's a huge bloom of red on his chest, and his gaze is fixed and staring up at nothing.

Leon—the man my wife calls Lee—is slumped forward, and I need to check on him, but Bianca is clinging to me so fiercely I can't let her go. Instead, I croon meaningless words into her hair and gently pat her back, keeping a watchful gaze on the shadows around us in the meantime.

Eventually, when she quiets down, I release her. "Where is our daughter?"

"Safe," she says. "I think. Especially now that he's dead."

She flicks her chin in the direction of Rossi's body.

"What happened? Did they shoot each other?"

I bend down to check the bodyguard's pulse, expecting nothing. My hand jerks slightly when I realize he's alive. I roll him to the side, and he groans and flutters his eyelids.

Bianca shrieks again and falls to her knees beside him. "Lee. I thought… I thought you were dead."

His eyes flicker open. "Can't put a good man down that easily."

He moans, and blood squelches as he tries to rise. He's bleeding pretty profusely from a shoulder wound.

"Stay down. We'll get you support as soon as we can." I speak into my ear mic, alerting Danelli to send in the waiting medical team the moment we have the area secured, and to send a man now to assist in staunching the blood as soon as one can be spared.

"And my daughter?" I ask Danelli. "I need an update."

I press my hands to the bodyguard's wound, placing pressure there until someone arrives to relieve me, while listening to Danelli's response.

I turn to Bianca, knowing she'll appreciate the news. "Emilia is safely away. They are being taken to a pre-arranged location to wait for us."

She slumps down beside me, clearly relieved at my words.

I frown at the crashed vehicle. "Theirs wasn't bulletproof, I see. A rookie mistake, and one that has obviously cost my enemy his life. So, what happened here?"

Bianca takes a deep breath and releases it in a rush. She shuffles over on her knees and molds her body into my side. I manage to contain my grunt of pain as she presses against my wound from the other night. The pain relief the doctor gave me would have made me sleepy, so I've barely taken any, and certainly none in the past twelve hours.

"I tried to shoot the driver, but I missed. So then Lee shot him, and the car crashed. Then Rossi got out and shot Lee. Then I shot Rossi."

"*You* killed Rossi?" I almost release my pressure on the bodyguard's shoulder in my shock.

"Yes. After he said… He said…" She shivers, the action so subtle I would not have felt it if she were not pressing so closely to my side.

"What did he say, Bianca?"

"He said he would make me watch while he chopped our daughter into little pieces and fed her to the sharks."

Sudden black edges my vision, and it is only the physical touch provided by Bianca at my side that keeps my rage in check. Until her next words tear my control to smithereens.

"He also said... I'm so sorry, Rio. But he said your parents discovered that Rina was still alive, so he and Rina killed them. And he said they did it..." A frightened-sounding little sob slips out of her mouth. "In my name."

Her words are like the final lift of a claw hammer against the simmering lid holding my rage in check.

With a roar, I rise to my feet as my vision darkens. While the faintest vestiges of mental coherence still remain, I stagger away from my wife, determined to put distance between us before my inner monster surfaces fully.

I do not want her to inadvertently get caught in the crossfire.

14

"I'm not afraid of storms, for I'm learning how to sail my ship."
Louisa May Alcott

Bianca

Iᴛ's lucky for Lee that one of Rio's men arrives at that moment and takes over placing pressure on his wound because Rio stiffened at my words, put me away from him, clamored to his feet, and stalked off into the shadows with a muted growl.

I want to run after him, call him back. Make sure he's okay. Because he sure as heck didn't look okay.

His face paled so much it could have been carved out of marble, but his eyes blazed, and even in the darkness, I saw a soullessness appear in his expression that I haven't seen in him before.

I don't chase him into the dark because I'm too scared of what he may do to me if I do.

I'm afraid, both *of* him and that blackness that mars his soul, and *for* him. Because he warned me about it, and while he's allowed me to see glimpses here and there, I've never seen him like this.

I know that darkness haunts him. I can guess the kind of things it makes him do.

So, instead of running after Rio, I stay with Lee, kneeling by his side and praying that Mitch really did get Emilia safely to whatever location Rio set up for us. I pray also for my husband, whose soul is so damaged that he cannot shake off the monster that rides him.

And in there, somewhere, I also pray for my birth mother. Not for her safety, but for her salvation. She is as dark and twisted as anyone else in this world, and the things she's done will probably send her straight to hell.

Like all of us.

I glance at Rossi's body, not as terrified about viewing the outcome of my actions as I was when I killed Penn. I can stare at his crumpled, blood-stained body with less angst than I expected.

Does killing become easier with every dead body that falls?

Somewhere deep down inside me, the screams I verbalized earlier are still raging rampant. *No. I am not okay with killing. I will never be okay with it.* Later, I will allow myself to fall apart. Right now, it is time to keep the panic at bay and stay focused. Stay calm. And stay in control, at all costs.

Because I suspect Rio is going to need me, and soon.

Then I remember what Rina said about someone working for her on the inside. I have to let Rio know.

I lean down, and as gently as I can, I remove Lee's ear mic. Before pressing it into my ear, I allow myself a tiny shudder, almost laughing at the irony of being squeamish about putting something from another person's ear into my own, when all around us there are wounded and bleeding and dead.

But I need to keep apprised of what's happening, and I need to speak with Rio, and with Lee drifting in and out of consciousness, he has no need of the tech at this point.

Instantly, I become connected to a larger group, voices talking and shouting and updating. I quickly realize that I can't say anything using the ear mic. The person who works for Rina is quite possibly connected to the comms, too. I'll have to tell Rio personally when I see him again, which will hopefully be soon.

The gunshots are only sporadic now, and I identify Danelli's voice when he says, "Everyone not assembled at the front entrance, report in."

There's a volley of voices, one after the other. Plenty of our men are still okay. Relief floods my system. Then Rio's second issues instructions for everyone still standing to make their way to the building where Rossi and Rina's captured crew members are being held.

"And send in the medics from the perimeter," he adds. "There is only one of our enemies left to contain, and she is likely long gone from here by now. Men are bleeding out. We need medics in here now."

One enemy, likely long gone. Rina. She got away? I stagger up to my feet, and sickness roils in my gut at the import of what that means for Emilia. And for Rio and me—if there still is a Rio and me after what I revealed just before he staggered off. Rina is obsessed with the Carlotti name, and she will never stop hunting us. Until either she ends up dead.

Or we do.

"Rio, no, wait... Ah, hell..." Nicky's voice in the earpiece contains more than a hint of concern.

And that terrifies me. Why is Nikolas, of all people, concerned?

Shots sound, one after the other, over and over and over, both in my earpiece and out loud, echoing through the night. I sink back down to my knees and hunch forward, hugging my belly. How many? How many has my husband just killed?

Please, Rio, no. Don't let it be true. Don't let the monster beat you...

Silence falls for the first time in what feels like hours, and I breathe heavily, letting tears fall unchecked down my cheeks before they drip off onto the ground.

Until a shocked whisper hisses through the earpiece from an unknown man, breaking the silence. "*Holy. Fuck. That was—*"

I rip the earpiece out and throw it to the ground, and then I drop my head into my hands and burst into tears at the knowledge that the complex man with whom I have fallen in love has been completely lost to the darkness.

Rio and I travel separately to his safe house, which turns out to be in Brookline on the outskirts of Boston. By the time I arrive there, accompanied by two goons whose names I don't know, dawn has already broken. The spring sky is still gray and heavy, and rain threatens—exactly matching my current mood.

The property is enormous, set in landscaped gardens with a long pool pavilion off to one side, and surrounded by trees that seem artfully placed for screening rather than having grown there naturally.

I can't begin to guess at the price tag of this place. A lot is all I know. The house itself is more modern than his riverside estate. The decor is Georgian style, painted white with charcoal trim, and features a long, single-level wing jutting off the main part of the imposing two-story house.

I haven't seen Rio since he lurched away from me in the darkness. I'm worried for him, but my first priority on arrival is finding and checking on Emilia.

Of course, Rio's need for controlling every detail means he has pre-arranged a nanny for her. When I enter the suite designated for my daughter, a middle-aged woman is on her knees blowing bubbles at Emilia from a little jar of liquid. Both of them are laughing.

She climbs to her feet and introduces herself as Susan. She has kind eyes and a ready smile, but she's still a stranger to me, and it will take some time before I trust anyone with my daughter.

Emilia is clearly safe and happy, with seemingly no ill effects from the drug Lee gave her at Rina's place. There is nothing for me to do but pick her up and hug her, inhaling her sweet scent, before placing her back down in her play pen where she resumes giggling at the bubbles.

"Your suite is next door, ma'am," Susan says as I hover, unsure what to do. "You can access it anytime through that door. It's lockable from your side only."

She points to the side of the room, and I nod gratefully when I see the door there is wide open. I'm pleased that I'll have twenty-four-seven access to Emilia.

"Thank you." I note the sympathy that lights her expression. She must have been told something about what happened.

For some reason, that knowledge fills me with shame, as if it were my fault that I allowed my daughter to be looked after by someone who ultimately kidnapped her.

"I, um... I need a shower. And then a nap, but I'll wait to sleep until Emilia is ready. Maybe... I think I'll have her in beside me while we sleep."

"Sure," Susan says easily, both of us pretending to ignore the anxiety that laced my statement. "I'd say she'll be ready for a nap in, say, an hour, ma'am?"

"Great. Thanks. That'll give me time to shower and explore the house a bit."

I want to ask her if Rio is here yet, but I'm too embarrassed to admit that the nanny may know more about my husband's whereabouts than I do, so in the end, I snap my mouth shut, nod at her again, and scurry through the connecting door into my suite.

In the privacy of the shower, under the steaming water, I finally allow out everything I've tried to tamp down up to this point. I sink to the tiled floor, rest my head on my knees, and let the tears fall.

The terror of not knowing if I'd ever see my daughter again. The shock of finding out my birth mother is alive—and that she's not only crazy, but evil. And that she killed my birth father, who may or may not have been equally monstrous. The escape out the window and through the trees in the dark, surrounded by gunfire and the threat of death. The fear for Lee, and then facing down Rossi...and killing him...

So much to process, and I don't even know how to start. Except to cry and cry and cry.

The thing that weighs heaviest on my mind, overshadowing everything else, is Rio. How could he simply go out there and shoot dead so many men, one after the other? In the heat of battle, or in a moment of defending himself or someone he loves…yes, I would understand that. Hell, I've done it now. Twice.

But to cold-bloodedly walk up to a bunch of kneeling men and execute them like that…

And that's exactly what he did. I asked one of the goons to explain what happened on the car ride here. He said "the boss" gave all the captured men the option to side with him, join the Agosti crew since Rossi was already dead.

Those who agreed, he spared. Those who spat on the ground at his feet, or swore to kill him and every member of his family, he shot, one after the other, until none of the dissenters were left.

Rossi's crew has been crushed into nothing by Rio, as effectively as he razed the man's homes and businesses. With Danelli, and Nicky, and countless others, to pick up the pieces afterward and tidy up his mess.

I hate what Rio is—he's a monster. He truly is.

I should hate *him*. Full stop. But I can't.

When I look deep down inside myself, I don't find any hate for Rio. I love him. I love him with all my heart, and I don't even know why. I just do. It feels as natural to me as breathing.

I'm not such a fool that I don't know what that makes me, too.

I'm not simply a monster's wife. I'm also a monster, at least as much as he is.

I wish with every cell of my being it were different for him, and for me. But it isn't.

I cry until there are no tears left in my body. And then I get to my feet, scrub myself all over, and step out of the shower. There is nothing to be done except keep moving forward, one step in front of the other, one moment at a time, one day at a time…and hope that the good parts of Rio have not been totally consumed by his darkness.

And that we can both be each other's salvation if we survive.

15

"*I don't believe the world's a particularly beautiful place, but
I do believe in redemption.*"
Colum McCann

Rio

I FINISH a lap in the long indoor pool and turn, launching into
another without pause. The pain in my side is burning
beneath the waterproof dressing, but I ignore it and focus on
my goal. Get to the other end of the pool, and then turn and
do it all again.

Over and over, until exhaustion takes over my mind, and
memories fade to gray.

I haven't reached that point yet. The memories from last
night, and from my past, are etched in my brain in stark
black-and-white clarity.

I am swimming now to tire the beast that lives within me.

Everyone thinks I love killing, but I don't. I hate it.

I hate it because every death—no matter how necessary—takes me back to that first time with my father. I always question what would have happened if I'd had the strength to stand up to him and simply say no.

It wouldn't have changed the outcome for the victim. My father would have done the kill, and then I'd likely be dead, too. Or cast out of the family as a failure, with Nicky taking my place as heir and favorite son.

I chose this path when I pulled that trigger for the very first time. Litle did I know back then that the act ignited the spark and created the monster I am known to be today.

Rossi's men had the opportunity to swear allegiance to my family. I gave them that choice. If they had done so, they would have lived. I made that clear.

By choosing not to, even knowing the consequences, they presented a threat to the Agosti family and empire, and I had no choice but to eliminate them.

Why the fuck didn't they all simply swear allegiance? I'd have found a place for them in my organization. And they wouldn't have died for nothing.

As I somersault at the deep end of the pool and launch into yet another lap, I become aware of someone watching me swim. I falter for a second, then keep going when I see it is Bianca who has entered at the other end of the pavilion. She stands with her arms folded across her middle and her hands gripping her elbows as she studies me.

I ignore her and keep swimming. I cannot face her revulsion.

Two more laps, keeping my head down, and then I hear a splash. Shocked, I stop mid stroke to see Bianca in the shallow end just ahead of me. Fully clothed. She is blocking my path to the wall. The water here is only a few feet deep, so both of us are able to stand.

I stare at her and take in her scowling expression. "What are you doing, Bianca?"

"Don't ignore me, Rio. I don't like it."

"Get out of the pool. Leave me alone. You need to—"

"No." She strides toward me, but if she's trying for elegance, the effect is hampered by the drag on her now-wet clothes that causes her to stagger. "I've waited all morning for you to come to me, and I'm sick of waiting. So here I am. And here you are, swimming back and forth for so long you're likely to sink under the surface and drown from sheer fatigue."

Finally, she reaches me and stares up into my face. I don't understand. I can't see any revulsion or hatred. That is the least I expected from her after what I did last night.

"Bianca, I don't know what to say to you. How to explain—"

"You don't have to say or explain anything if you don't want to." She launches at me, wrapping her arms around my waist and holding on tightly.

The action is so unexpected I stagger, and I realize she's correct in one thing at least. I'm about to drop from exhaustion.

"I love you, Rio." Her words are muffled against my wet skin.

My heart skips a beat. "How can you love me? Now that I've shown my true colors…"

Sadness fills me for what might have been with this woman, and to my horror, my eyes begin to burn. It can't be from chlorine or salt because this is mineral-laced pool water.

No. I grit my teeth. *Rio Agosti does. Not. Cry.*

I must be allergic to the magnesium.

The hitching of my breath must give me away because she peels back and stares up again. Her own eyes fill with moisture at whatever she reads in my expression.

"One day I'm going to help you conquer that inner demon," she says quietly, and in this moment, I know I will never love another the way I love this woman.

She sees me. She sees the monster within, and she isn't running. Not anymore.

I open my mouth to respond when her gaze shifts beyond me, and she stiffens.

"Get out!" She shouts the words, and I hear a sharp inhale behind me.

I start to turn, despite the moisture leaking from my eyes, but she holds me in place. Trying to protect my reputation?

"Make sure no one else enters until one of us gives the okay. Is that clear?"

A mumbled male voice says, "Yes, ma'am," and then the pavilion door closes with a snick.

I sink down beneath the water to cleanse my face, inadvertently taking her with me.

When we resurface, she is spluttering and laughing. "A little notice next time would be good!"

I smooth the locks of hair that have gone everywhere back off her face and kiss her forehead before I state my intention. "The real me surfaced last night. The one I never wanted to show you. If you wish, I will release you from our marriage vows. I will let you go, Bianca. You and Emilia. Is that what you want?"

Her eyes widen, and her mouth drops open. "You would do that, for me and Emilia?"

"Yes. I have come to love you, *mia cara*, more than anything in this world. But you deserve better than being shackled to someone like me."

"What if I *want* someone like you? What if I want...*you*?"

Surely, she can't truly mean that. "Do you?"

She punches me on the arm. "Of course I fucking do! You're my husband, Rio, and I've grown to love you, too. Despite who you are at your core." She frowns. "Or maybe because of it? I just love *you*, and that includes all of you, good and bad. What you did last night was..."

She shudders in the water, and the ripples fan out around us. "It was awful. We both know that, but we all did awful things last night. I killed another human being. I killed *Rossi*! A man I thought of as a friend of sorts! We've both done awful things at other times, too."

The brightness in her eyes dims, and I know she's thinking of Penn, the nanny. Perhaps also of her old friends from the animal shelter. She confided in me a few months ago that she felt a lot of guilt over what happened to them and how she'd treated them afterward.

I want to comfort her, tell her it will be all right. But that is not always the truth in this life. She continues before I can formulate a sentence that doesn't reek of lies.

"It doesn't change how I feel about you, Rio. You're it for me. You and Emilia. And any other children, if we're lucky enough one day to have more."

I can barely breathe. No one has ever seen the real me as thoroughly and completely as she has. And yet, she accepts me regardless of what she sees.

"You surprise me more every single day, Bianca."

Pleasure flares in her eyes. "Good. I like surprising you."

113

We drift in the water, floating farther down toward the deep end, and I try to analyze what I'm feeling. When Bianca is in my vicinity, she brings light with her. Light instead of dark. Hope instead of the rage I've grown used to nurturing.

She suddenly flails, as if realizing she's floated out of her depth while still fully clothed.

I pull her in and hold her more firmly. "Relax. I've got you, Bianca. I can still reach the bottom here. Though it might be a good idea to lose some of this clothing. You are overdressed for the occasion."

"I didn't come in here with the intention of jumping in."

"I didn't think so."

"Will you help me? Remove my clothing?"

A rush of desire heads straight to my cock. "With pleasure."

At least she left her shoes at the side of the pool. I lift her up to sit on the pool's paved edge, and then between us, we shuck off her pants and the tiny pair of bright-pink panties that barely covers her mound. She lifts her sweater over her head and dumps it on the sodden pile of clothing now behind her before releasing and throwing her bra aside, too.

Her exposed nipples are erect, her breasts still lush and full from breastfeeding, even though she is no longer able to do that. The rose-tipped flesh calls for my mouth, but I have something better in mind. She starts to slide back down into the water, but I stop her with a firm hand on her belly.

"Not so fast."

"But—"

"This is the perfect position for a feast."

"A feast?"

I grin, allowing all the hunger pulsing through my body to

114

show in my expression, and then I push her legs wide, exposing her bare pussy to my view. She is beautiful, so perfect.

And she's all *mine*.

I lean in and begin to eat my fill.

16

"There is no end. There is no beginning. There is only the passion of life."
Federico Fellini

Bianca

Rio FEASTS on my pussy like a starving man, licking and kissing and tasting all the way up and down my seam before catching my clit with his lips. He circles the bud with his tongue, and I gasp as awareness ripples outward and infuses my whole body with heat.

"Oh, Rio. That feels so...*good!*" I lean back a little, resting on my hands, feeling boneless and languid and not in control as he lifts my legs and repositions them over his strong shoulders.

"You like?" His words vibrate against my clit, and I shudder and thrust my hips upward, instinctively looking for more.

"I love."

Then his mouth leaves my core, and he licks and nibbles along my inner thighs. First on the right, almost down to my knee, then back up to brush over my pussy lips before heading down my left thigh and back up. While his mouth explores, his fingertips stay on target, stroking along my seam before finding and teasing my channel entrance.

He pushes in with one finger, then a second, and I moan at the exquisite sensation of him inside me at the same time as his thumb is stroking my clit.

My breathing becomes ragged and harsh as desire ramps up. When his mouth returns to my core and he holds me open so he can dip inside me with his tongue, I arch up and into him, needing everything he has to give. Needing more.

His tongue… His fingers… It's not enough…

As if he can sense exactly how much I'm craving, he steps back, mouth still eating me out while he brings me into the water with him. Finally, he raises his head and stares up my floating body with an expression that leaves no room for misinterpretation.

Rio is hungry for me. And he is only just getting started.

His lips are slightly swollen, shiny and damp from his feast, and if I could summon the strength, I would reach up and swipe my thumb across them and bring my own taste to my mouth. But I'm too achy with desire, too much in need. Instead, I spread my arms out to the sides and float.

My legs are still splayed wide, but now hang over his elbows instead of his shoulders. His hands cradle my lower back, helping to keep me atop the water without any effort on my part.

It doesn't seem fair that I receive all the pleasure.

"I want to touch you, too, Rio. I want to feel your hardness in my hands before you fuck me."

He kicks a little beneath me, bringing us closer to the shallow end. When he stops, he releases me, and I find I can stand easily here. He takes both of my hands in his and brings them to his cock that is already standing to attention.

"Touch me, then, wife. As much as you like."

I laugh lightly as I run my hands up and down his silken hardness. "When did you lose your swimming trunks?"

He chuckles, too. "While you took off your sweater. You know I'm into managing time effectively."

The words may be logical, but the raspy tone in which he utters them is not, and his flesh jerks in my hands as I wrap my fingers around him and pull.

"Little bird, you do know how to arouse me."

I rub my thumb over the head of his cock, enjoying his size and the small groan my action elicits from him. Even in the water, I can tell he's leaking pre-cum. There's a difference in the consistency beneath my thumb tip. He is clearly enjoying what I'm doing.

I squeeze him a little and pull again, and he shudders and releases another groan, this one louder than the last. Immediately after that sound, he grabs me and drags me closer, leaning in to claim my mouth in a kiss that tastes both of Rio and myself, laced with the clean tang of minerals from the pool water.

I love kissing this man. His lips and tongue and teeth are so sure on mine, coaxing a response that comes from deep down within me. I wrap my legs around his hips and my arms around his neck, tangling my fingers in his dark hair.

Wanting to be as close as possible in every way.

I don't realize I'm writhing against him, rubbing my pussy in a frenzied fashion on his belly, until his hands clasp my hips to steady me.

"I am not going to fuck you, Bianca."

"Oh *no*! But—"

"I am going to *make love* with you. Claim you as mine. Now and forever."

With those words, he pulls me down onto his cock, thrusting upward with his hips at the same time and seating himself deep within me. My channel clenches around him as if it will never let him go. The feeling of completeness is beautiful, and it pushes me right to the edge of orgasm before he even moves.

I tilt back my head and close my eyes, concentrating only on the amazing feeling of undulating my pelvis and riding him, hard. Overlaid with the feel of *him* riding *me*, pumping into my body slowly at first, and then faster, until there is nothing left but Rio and me, riding each other in this bubble of perfection…

I shatter in his arms, jerking and screaming as he roars and releases into me at the exact same moment, in a mutual climax that goes on and on and on.

Finally, when I come back to earth, I discover I'm sobbing against him, my head snuggled in the crook of his neck. He is stroking my back, murmuring soft words in Italian into my wet hair. I look up and see moisture leaking again from his eyes, as it was when I sent that intruder packing earlier. But this time he doesn't seem embarrassed or try to hide it from me.

Instead, we cling together, weeping, in a shared moment of emotional closeness and beauty that we both know is only fleeting. The world and its monsters—our own and those of many others—still wait for us outside that door.

WE USE the shower room in the pool pavilion to clean up, and I dress in one of the neatly folded fluffy white robes on offer. When I start to head over to my pile of sodden clothing, Rio stops me with a shake of his head.

"I'll have the housekeeper sort that out. Come. We need some sleep."

He's right. I only had a few hours' sleep at Rina and Rossi's place, and I'm guessing Rio has had even less than that.

He leads me back to my suite, and a thrill of pleasure runs through me when I check it out properly and see his clothing is also sitting in the dressing room. I hadn't noticed when I was in here earlier, as the sweater and jeans I donned had already been laid out for me on the ottoman at the end of the king-sized bed.

"This is your suite, too? We're in here together?"

One of his brows rises. "Of course. Unless you prefer we sleep separately?"

"No. I'm pleased. Really pleased." I tug him over to the bed.

When I'm wrapped in his arms, I remember what I needed to tell him. I half sit up and turn to him, but he's already asleep, dark circles of exhaustion beneath his closed eyelids.

I sink back down and lie still. He needs the rest, so I'll tell him as soon as he wakes. Soon I, too, fall into sleep, wrapped in my husband's embrace.

When I wake, he's staring down at me, a tiny smile lifting his lips. I don't want to destroy the moment of closeness, but I have to let him know.

"Rio, when I was with Rina and Rossi, she said something you need to know."

His smile disappears, and his gaze sharpens into focus. "Yes?"

"She said, 'we have someone working with us,' and I took it to mean she has someone here in your organization, working to bring you down from the inside. Rossi shut the conversation down fast before I could find out more."

Rio sits up in bed and stares at me, tapping a finger on his bottom lip in a thoughtful gesture. "If that is true, then it won't matter where we go to hide. They will have intel on this place already."

I sit up too and hug my raised knees. "So, we're not safe here, either? Do we need to move Emilia again?"

My heart sinks. This place feels nice, and the thought of continually moving, never settling until Rina is stopped, fills me with dread.

"I will consider what needs to be done. But if they know of this place, they will know anywhere we go. And here has a few hidden extras that my riverside estate didn't have that will help with keeping the property secure. Did she give any indication who it might be?"

I shake my head regretfully. "I wish I'd gotten more from her. I'm sorry."

"No matter." He slides out of bed and moves to the window, staring out before turning back to face me.

I know my news has thrown him because his expression is firmly shuttered. I'm beginning to understand he does that to hide when his emotions are running high.

"Until we know more, do not trust anyone, Bianca. Except me, of course. And Angel and Nicky. Do not go anywhere with any of the bodyguards unless there are at least three of them."

"Three? Isn't that a bit of overkill?"

"If Rina has one person on the inside, she could equally have commandeered one of my security pairs. It is widely known that Danelli sets up my security in that way. So, three with you from now on as an added precaution."

"All right. But…Angel and Nicky? They're not here, are they?"

He grins at me then, and for a moment, he seems to lose the grim exterior. "Not yet. But they will be here later today. I was going to tell you about our incoming guests before you distracted me earlier in the pool."

My heart lifts at the news, particularly in relation to Angel. "I've missed her. I'm glad she's coming. I mean, that *they're* coming," I correct in the interest of fairness.

Nicky isn't all horrible.

"I want all close members of my family here while we regroup and work out our next moves. I'd have recalled Francine's son, too, but Tommaso is overseas at present dealing with an issue in one of my Mediterranean enterprises. He prefers to keep busy since his mother passed and was happy to be given that task."

As Rio dresses in black pants and one of his seemingly obligatory white silk shirts, I sit up and slide out of bed, both pleasure and regret rising within me. Regret that our nightmare isn't yet over and the real world is intruding far too soon. And pleasure at the thought of seeing Angel again.

"When will they arrive?"

He glances at his watch. "In about an hour. Just in time for a family dinner."

I rush into the dressing room, calling over my shoulder, "I'd like to make a meal for us all. And could we eat in the kitchen for once, instead of more formally? I had a look when I first arrived and explored the house. That kitchen is bigger than any apartment I've ever lived in, and yet it still has a lovely feel. Homely."

A snort from the other room reaches my ears, then he says, "We have a cook. She can prepare something for us."

My shoulders slump. Of course there's a cook. Rio has everyone and everything at his beck and call. So much for my plan to cook *for* him.

"But if you wish to eat informally, then we can certainly accommodate that," he says, as if sensing my disappointment. "Our family has never before dined in the kitchen, Bianca. It will be interesting to see what Angel and Nikolas make of the experience."

I finish dressing and return to the bedroom. Rio smiles at me with an indulgent air, but I can see the cogs turning in his mind. I know he's still half focused on trying to figure out who the internal traitor may be.

17

"A happy family is but an earlier heaven."
George Bernard Shaw

Rio

"Bianca! Oh, it's so good to see you!"

Angel's voice as she greets my wife pulls me out of reading through a contract Carnarvon has sent for my signature. I am having trouble concentrating, following Bianca's revelation about a possible mole.

Most of my crew have been with me for many years, and any more recent placements have been vetted to within an inch of their lives by Danelli and Carnarvon's teams.

I rub my eyes, exhausted with my thoughts swirling round and round, considering everyone in my employ. This is not the time to lose hold of the reins, even for a second. The enemy is still out there, possibly a lot closer than I expected, so I need to maintain control now more than ever.

I place the contract back on my desk and head out of my

office into the foyer of the house to see my sister and wife embracing as tightly as if they are a lifeline for one another.

Perhaps they are. It has been a difficult time for everyone. I'm glad Angel and Bianca can be of comfort to each other.

Eventually they pull apart, and my sister sees me watching them. She squeals and rushes over to hug me, too. "Rio. I've been so worried about you. I'm glad you told Nicky to bring me here. It's good to be with you and Bianca at the moment. And I know you'll keep us safe here."

My heart squeezes a little at her words. I will do my utmost to keep them all safe. In truth, this property is not foolproof, whether or not there is a traitor within our midst. Nowhere is truly safe from those, like me, who have enough power and money to blast a path through other people's secrets. But it is as safe as I can make it. For now.

The layout of the grounds is easier to monitor than the riverside estate, and cameras cover most of the acreage as well as within the house itself. The land is more compact and less forested than that of my other estates, and there is no river access to be concerned about.

The number of men I have stationed here, both in and around the house itself, and throughout the grounds, is more than I have ever called upon for personal security before. And it is now being supplemented by Martelli.

But I would be a fool not to acknowledge that nowhere is really safe from Rina Carlotti and those who support her. Not until she is dead and buried. Six feet under.

I scowl at the thought of that woman and her far-reaching impact on our lives, just as Nicky staggers in through the front entrance. He's loaded up with bags, which he drops on the floor next to a smaller pile that Angel has obviously recently abandoned.

"You look irritated," he says. "Which is ironic because you're not the one fetching and carrying. *I* am." He shrugs out his shoulders and groans. "We traveled economy."

I raise my brow at him. "You came by car. Easier to avoid being tracked than a flight would have been."

"Yeah. Still. No valet service this trip. Only the driver, who left the moment he dumped the last bag on the ground out front."

"One of Martelli's men."

His Washington crew are obviously not as inclined to "fetch and carry" for my family as much as one of my own men would have done. It is a reminder that I need to have a conversation with Nicky about what Martelli's support means. But that can wait until after dinner.

"Come, then. I'll show you to your rooms. And"—I gesture for him to follow me—"I will arrange someone—a valet, of sorts—to carry your bags so you do not need to exert yourself any further."

"Thanks, brother." He comes closer and slaps me on the back. "It's good to see you, Rio. Are you all right, after…"

He waves a hand, the curiosity in his eyes obvious. He must be referring to what happened at Rossi's estate, and the last thing I wish to do right now is discuss that debacle.

"I am fine. Bianca," I call out, more harshly than I mean to.

She looks up from her conversation with Angel and frowns a little.

"Show Angel to her rooms. I've put her upstairs, on the far side of Emilia's suite. Nicky, you're this way."

I lead him through the wide entryway and connecting hallway that leads to the single level add-on. This section used to be a separate carriage house, I've been told, but it was

126

renovated prior to my purchase to bring it in as part of the main house. Perfect for my brother, who will no doubt appreciate the privacy of his own guest wing.

Not that he'll be able to entertain private guests anytime soon. This location is on a need-to-know basis, and Nicky's women can wait for his return to the city. I will need to have *that* conversation with him, too.

"Get comfortable, and then meet us in the kitchen in an hour or so for dinner."

"All right—wait. The *kitchen*?"

"Bianca's idea. I'm indulging her."

His eyes widen a little before he grins. "Of course you are. Well, it'll be an interesting experience, I'm certain."

Bianca

RIO SAID he hadn't ventured into the kitchen of any of his homes since he was a boy. Luckily, this one has a cheerful vibe as we gather around the small, eight-seat wooden table on one side of the huge square space.

Despite being early evening and still only spring, the clouds outside have cleared, and there is dappled sunlight coming through the windows that look out on part of the manicured garden. Around the edge of the room are marble countertops with cupboards beneath, and dominating the middle of the space is a large square area with a copper exhaust above a cooktop and more counter space.

The cook, Mrs. Jarvis, who I met earlier when I explored the house, has left salads and wine out on the central counter area and a beef casserole warming in the oven. She has already made herself scarce. Everyone in the house seemed as shocked as Rio was when I told them to set the table for dinner in here and not the dining room.

"This is fun," Angel says, clapping her hands before taking a seat opposite Nicky. "Like a picnic."

I secure Emilia into her high chair and then turn to give Rio a grin. "Take a seat. I'll bring everything over."

I pour wine and hand Angel a soda, studiously ignoring her side-eye at the lack of alcohol, then bring over the salads and the casserole to the table, taking the time while they're all serving themselves to feed Emilia her bowl of pureed pear.

It is a domestic-bliss kind of scene that could be found in many households throughout America, and yet underlying our surface enjoyment lurks the ever-present darkness. I can't escape it, now that I know it exists, and neither can any one of us at the table.

But my purpose this evening is to try and bring some light to Rio's life and remind him that there are simple pleasures worth fighting for, beyond the amassing of power, wealth, and prestige.

Angel, predictably, dominates the conversation, telling Rio and me what it was like living overseas at her finishing school and how glad she is to be back here where she belongs, with her family.

"Probably safer over there than here, Angel," Nicky says dryly.

She shrugs and swallows a mouthful of food before answering. "It was certainly more interesting than staying with you, Nicky. I thought we'd have fun in the city, even though we were hiding there to avoid what was happening at the estate. But no. You kept me under lock and key, and you didn't even have any books for me to read to while away the time."

"You had your phone. There're always digital books," he counters.

The two continue to bicker gently, while I finish feeding Emilia and fetch her bottle, and then I eat too while Rio watches me, warmth lighting his expression and a funny little smile lifting the corners of his lips.

"You okay?" I mouth at him, and his smile widens briefly.

"I am very okay," he says quietly.

Nicky and Angel stop talking and stare at their brother, then over at me.

"Well," Nicky says. "I think we all might be okay."

There are multiple layers of meaning in those words. For the first time since meeting him, I sense Nicky's growing acceptance of me as part of this family. Warmth spreads out in my chest, and when Emilia makes a little burping noise, a laugh bursts out of me unbidden.

"Feels like a real family," Angel says, and I notice there are sudden tears in her eyes.

"We *are* a real family," I counter. "Have you really never done this before? Just…hung out together, with no agenda other than to eat? And chat?"

I look from her, to Nicky, and finally, to Rio, not fully understanding their personal history even though I'm aware their family history is steeped in crime and violence.

From the snippets Rio has let slip since I've known him, it sounds like their father was abusive and cold. But what of their mother? What of Francine and their cousin Tommaso, who must have been around at least some of the time when they were all growing up?

All of them answer me at once.

129

"No, we have not," Rio says.

"Hell no. Why would we do that?" Nicky asks.

"Our parents were scary, and they barely spoke to us." That last statement comes from Angel, who is blinking hard and clearly trying not to cry. "Father didn't like us, and if we ever made any noise, we'd be punished. Rio always more so than me or Nick, as he was the oldest and had to be perfect 'cause he was the heir."

I glance at Rio's suddenly impassive face. He's staring at Emilia. *His* heir.

When he notices me looking, his lips twist. "I will never treat our daughter that way."

I reach over and touch his arm, stroking the taut muscles lightly. "I know," I say, with truth lacing my tone.

He won't be abusive toward Emilia. Or toward me. Not now that he's discovered love. I cringe a little at my soppy thoughts, but they're true. I just know, with every fiber of my being, that Rio would die before he deliberately hurt either one of us.

I wouldn't have said that when we first married. But I know it in my heart now as the truth.

"Father was just plain terrifying," Angel adds. "Even Mother was scared of him. When he was in a rage…"

She shudders and lifts her soda to take a sip. Then she glances at Rio before looking down at her plate, and we all hear the unspoken words. *Like you, Rio.*

Except, I think, there's a difference between Rio and his father. My husband now has me in his corner. Me and Emilia. And I refuse to allow that darkness to completely swallow him up.

Nicky shifts in his chair, as if uncomfortable with the turn of conversation. "We'll all be singing "Kumbaya" next. Or playing Scrabble," he pipes up, and for some reason, that strikes us all as funny.

Even Rio chuckles and shakes his head.

The slight tension that had entered the room at the mention of their father dissipates to nothing, and I clear the table and serve up the pecan pie and ice cream left by Mrs. Jarvis before the evening finally comes to a close.

The cook left a note on top of the pie that read: *Please, Mrs. Agosti. Let me do my job. Leave the cleaning up to me.*

I am very happy to take her up on that offer.

"Nicky, I need a word in my office," Rio says, standing. The family camaraderie is clearly over. "There is something I must discuss with you regarding Gianni Martelli."

"Sure." Nicky's brows furrow in obvious puzzlement, but he follows Rio out of the kitchen, leaving me with Angel and Emilia, who is falling asleep in her chair.

I unclip her, lift her up into my arms, and walk upstairs with Angel by my side.

"Bianca, you're making a positive difference to Rio," Angel says when we stop outside Emilia's suite. "He's still the head of the family, and everyone can see the heavy weight that places on his shoulders, but since he got you back, and this little one came into our lives..." She gently taps Emilia on the nose, then leans in to give her a kiss atop her head. "He's different. Less like our father. Less frightening."

Is that a good thing for a Mafia boss? I open and close my mouth, unsure of what to say.

Angel laughs lightly and turns, as if she can read my thoughts, "It's a good thing, Bianca. Believe me. You are perfect for one another."

"And you"—I bump her with my free shoulder—"are a very perceptive young woman. For a nineteen-year-old."

"Hey," she protests. "None of that ageist stuff. I'm smart and perceptive for *any* age."

"That you are, hon. And I'm so glad you're here."

As we say good night and part ways, I reflect on the journey that Rio and I have taken to get to this point. From kidnapping and forced marriage, to love and family. With death and violence in between.

I can only pray that my birth mother—the only blood family I have left outside these walls—does not come swanning in to destroy it all, before we find and destroy her first.

18

"In the beginning it was all black and white."
Maureen O'Hara

Bianca

I WIDEN my stance and hold the Glock as steady as I can while waiting for the beep. When the *go* signal sounds, I aim at the shadowy figure at the end of the tunnel and squeeze the trigger, several times, before lowering the weapon and placing it on the shelf in front of me.

"Reload the way I showed you." Rio's voice comes from directly behind me.

I pick up the gun and remove the magazine, then adjust the slide before refilling the magazine with bullets. "Like this?"

"Yes. Keep it pointing that way, down the range, and just tilt it like this." Rio's hands cover mine as he shows me what to do.

I load, and then he makes me unload again, ensuring I pop

out the bullet in the chamber as well to make the weapon safe.

I place the gun back into an ornate case, which Rio says is now mine but will need to be stored in the safe upstairs in our suite.

I stroke the lid of the case, enjoying the filigreed pattern of the metal that decorates the lid.

When I asked him if he'd teach me how to shoot properly, I never expected him to open a door just inside the entrance of the single-story guest wing where Nicky is currently staying and lead me down a set of stairs to an underground firing range.

"Did this come ready-made with the house?" I asked him dryly, staring wide-eyed at the row of booths with paper targets waiting at the end of each long corridor.

"What do you think?" His tone was equally dry, and I had to laugh.

"I think you had it installed after you bought it. No one normal just randomly happens to have a shooting range inside their home."

He simply grinned at me and then led me through to what he called the armory room to retrieve a weapon and ammunition for my use.

"We'll start with the Glock 19 today," he said. "Given that's the one you're most familiar with."

The one I shot Penn with, he meant, but I shook my head. "No. I want to try the one I took from Lee. It was harder to use. It kicked so much I missed the driver of that car altogether. I want to be able to protect myself, and Emilia, if you or the goons are ever not here and there's a threat."

He paused and then shook his head. "Not today. Glock

first, just to get used to the range. Then you can try another type of pistol tomorrow if you want to."

I pouted, but he was adamant. And I have to admit, the feel of the Glock in my hand and the heady moment of shooting at something not alive have given me a huge thrill. Maybe I'll just accept the Glock 19 is *my* weapon and use it every time I need to protect myself.

Hopefully that won't happen often.

The heat of Rio's body close behind me is a comfort, and I take a step back and lean into him, lowering my ear protectors and swiveling to face my husband.

"Can I please see how I did?"

"Certainly." His tone is indulgent. "Take those goggles off first, and then push this button here. It will reel in your target."

Oh. I must look ridiculous, staring up at him in these things. I lift the goggles and rest them atop my head, sunglasses-style, then turn back and do as he says. I wait until the paper target with the person silhouetted in the middle of the circle gets close.

"Damn." I release a sigh. "I'd be dead if that had been a real person."

Most of the bullet holes pepper the white paper around the figure.

"This one possibly would have been a kill shot." He taps the one hole that just skims the top of the person's head. "Not bad for your first effort, Bianca. Well done."

"Thank you." Who would have ever thought I'd be pleased to receive praise from someone about having a successful kill shot?

Shooting a gun down here in the firing range, with paper figures as targets, is vastly different from what happened up there in the real world. With real people who got hurt and killed far too easily.

"There was something about watching you when you pointed your weapon at that target and aimed…"

I blink and do a double take. Is that what I think it is in Rio's tone? I drop my gaze and realize it is. He's sporting a healthy-looking hard-on.

"You are an extremely sexy woman, little bird. Especially when you focus on hitting your target."

"I…err…" I open and close my mouth.

Now that he mentions it, there was something extremely empowering about taking control of my own security. And when Rio is standing there, staring at me with blatant desire in his expression…

I feel unaccountably shy all of a sudden. "I've never made love in a shooting range before."

"Good. I cannot say it is something I've ever done either. Until now."

He steps forward and shifts the gun case to one side of the cubicle shelf and then turns me so I'm facing away from him toward the target area once again. When he presses against my rear, his erection nudges my butt.

"This is going to be quick and dirty, my wife. But I promise, we will do slow and sensual later, in our marital bed."

Rio

QUICK AND DIRTY is all I can manage. I can barely hold on to my control long enough to unzip my pants and lift the hem of her dress.

She's wearing skimpy black panties beneath, and I slide the fingers of each hand beneath the edges and rip them in two. Not required. They drift to the floor somewhere behind us.

Her gasp echoes around the range, amplified in the small space.

"Spread your legs." I nudge her thighs apart with my knee and then position my ready cock at her entrance. She leans forward, gripping the edge of the cubicle shelf, and angles her butt in such a way that it forces the tip of me inside her.

Heat. Wet. Divine.

I pull back, determined to last longer than a kid enjoying his first-ever fuck.

Her pussy is so ready for me even without any foreplay. It is almost as if the act of watching her aim at that target was the actual foreplay for both of us.

I could barely keep my hands off her while she wielded that gun. The way she focused so intently on the target. The way her top teeth nibbled at her bottom lip while she concentrated. The hitching of her breath that jutted her beautiful breasts forward in an innocently provocative pose. The curve of her ass cheeks presenting to me, as if begging for my cock to shove deep and hard between them.

The way she held that weapon with both hands, gripping just the way I showed her, not too tight but with just enough control to coax the weapon to do her bidding...

My cock leaks pre-cum, desperate to finish despite my brain's determination to last at least a few more minutes.

Fuck, I want her. So bad. I thrust forward, dipping into her wet heat for an inch or two before pulling out again. I groan into the back of her neck at the exquisite sensation of her channel trying to suck me farther in.

Fucking my wife is like finally finding my way home. I can't get enough of her.

Her breath becomes rasping and uneven, the sound on the edge of a moan, and her hips wriggle against my crotch until I grab her and hold her still.

"No, Bianca. Let me do this my way." I thrust in again, giving her a couple more inches this time, and the muscles of her channel clench around me so tightly I almost lose my load right there and then.

I pull out again, her juices coating me, and tease her with my cock head by stroking forward along her seam to find the swollen bud of her clit and press it with my tip, and then I slide back, all the way up to the rosebud of her ass, before moving forward again.

"You said quick and dirty," she moans, her words hoarse and her tone accusing. "I need you inside me, Rio."

"I did say that," I whisper against her skin.

The scent of her rises around me, and I lick the back of her neck, tasting desire. Tasting her readiness.

She is slick and in need. And now it is time to deliver.

I pump into her, hard, all the way to the hilt, and she drops her head back and releases a guttural sound that vibrates against my chest. I thrust again, and then I give her what I promised. Quick and hard and dirty.

I drill into her, moving fast, propelling her forward until the edge of the shelf adds pressure to her clit as I pump her from behind.

The thump-thump-thump of our bodies slapping against each other fills the range, her moans and groans mingling with mine, and then there's the telltale stiffening of her back and its involuntary arch as she reaches the cliff edge of climax and begins to topple over with a mangled-sounding scream.

I continue to pound into her, carrying her over the edge with me and releasing a roar as we fall together into the blessed oblivion of a mutual orgasm.

An orgasm fueled by the smell of gunpowder and surrounded by spent bullet casings.

"Life is not what you expect. It is made up of the most unexpected twists and turns."
Ilaiyaraaja

Bianca

ANGEL THREADS her arm through mine as we stroll around the grounds of the estate. Three goons trail behind us, as ordered by Rio, but at least he gave permission for us to leave the house, as long as we stay within the perimeter, which is ringed by these thick trees and shrubs.

No riverfront here, and no views other than what is visible in the gardens, but it feels good to get outside and allow fresh air on my face.

Angel tugs on my elbow. "This reminds me of that walk around Boston, when we pretended to be tourists. That was a fun day," she says, and I smile in memory.

"It *was* good. Until the Feds showed up and ruined it."

I wonder what happened to Felicity, the agent who tried to

get me to turn on Rio and his family. She didn't seem the type to accept money or a bribe, but I suspect someone in her team was less law-abiding. She was probably assigned to a whole different case, in the end.

I'm glad, because I think she would have been quite a tenacious opponent if she'd been allowed to continue investigating the Agosti organization.

"True. We'll have to finish that walk one day, Bianca. Let's make a promise to each other to do it when things settle down again."

My pulse gives a little skip at the thought of such a normal activity, and then reality kicks back in, and the excitement skitters away. I no longer live a "normal" life, and there is no guarantee of things ever fully settling down.

"I'd love to finish that walk, Angel. When things settle."

Will they ever? Or will we live like this for the rest of our lives, hiding out from my birth mother, or other so-far-unidentified enemies, moving from one of Rio's secret homes to another every time one of his properties is breached?

Yes, I tell myself, trying to stop the spiraling worry before it takes off and becomes panic. Of course things will settle. We *will* be safe one day. And I *will* finish that damn tourist walk with Angel.

"I promise," I say, and she sighs happily.

We've been here in this safe house for over a week now, and both of us are going stir crazy. Before I met Rio, I worked full-time in the animal shelter, and this sitting around doing nothing is driving me mad. I know Angel is practically bouncing off the walls, too, so this walk around the grounds of the estate will do us both good.

The days are starting to get longer, the weather warming up a touch, and today the sun has broken through the clouds.

It is quite pleasant to be out here among the trees, just wandering aimlessly.

I glance back at the goons on duty today. I don't know any of them by name, but they're only here to accompany us for the walk. When we head back into the house, another trio will take over.

Lee is recovering well from his gunshot wound to the shoulder, but it will be some time before he's allowed back on duty. If ever. The bullet tore up some vital muscles and tendons, apparently, so Rio said he'll need a lot of rehab to get his body back to full health.

"What will he do for money?" I asked Rio when he mentioned it a couple of days ago. "How will he—"

"We look after our own, Bianca. Leon and his family will be well looked after, until such time as he is able to return to work. And if he is not able to return at all, then a pension arrangement will be set up for him."

"Okay. That sounds good." The care aspect of this life is one I'm still getting used to.

There may be death and violence and killing galore, but for those in Rio's family, or his crew, he is honor-bound to take care of them should something happen in the line of duty.

"What are your names?" I call out to the goons trailing behind us. Then a horrific thought strikes. "None of you is called...Leon, by any chance?"

I'm becoming a bit superstitious about that name.

"I'm John, ma'am," the taller one says politely.

"And my name is Tony," says a shorter, dark-haired one.

"Santo, ma'am," the third one says. He's blond, but judging by his accent and the name, I suspect the color comes from a dye job rather than being natural.

All three of them are muscled and hard-looking, and not making any attempt to hide the weapons in their shoulder holsters.

"Oh, good. Well, nice to meet you, John, Tony, and Santo. We'll just do another circuit of the grounds before we head back inside."

"Yes, ma'am," John says. "Take as long as you need."

We thread our way through a section of garden that contains a mass planting of roses and head through an arbor covered with vines into an area filled with apple trees.

"Oh, I didn't know this was here," I say, staring around. "Some of these apples actually look ready to pick."

"What's that?" Angel asks, dropping her grip on my arm and pointing through the trees.

I squint, seeing a dark lump of something indefinable on the ground up ahead. "Not sure."

My heart picks up pace, and worry knots my stomach. That doesn't look like a random pile of trash. It looks like…

I start toward it, walking fast, even though part of me wants to run the other way. Angel is right on my heels, until a strong hand grabs my arm and pulls me to a halt.

"Ma'am, wait." It is Tony, the shorter goon. He has also grabbed Angel in his other hand.

Like Angel and me, all three goons are staring at the lump up ahead.

I gasp, my brain finally conceding what I'm looking at. "That's a body."

"Stone-cold dead, by the looks of it," Angel says.

Despite her flippant words, her tone contains horror, and her hands have risen to cover her mouth.

John is already speaking urgently into his ear mic, telling

someone to inform the boss, then directing Tony to get us back to the house.

"Pronto!" he barks as Santo pulls his gun and scans the orchard with a narrowed gaze.

I resist Tony's pull on my arm.

"No. I need to see who it is." I can't even tell if it's male or female. What if it's Rina? That would end the threat against us, of course, but the thought of my birth mother lying there in the grass like a piece of tossed-out garbage…

I rip my arm out of Tony's grip and run toward the body, tuning out his and John's curses as I go.

I have to see. I have to know for sure.

I stop short when I reach it, my breath choppy with fear. Not Rina. The matted hair is blonde, not dark like hers. But I can tell it is a woman. Or rather, it was.

She's wearing jeans and a black leather jacket, and I have a horrible sick feeling in my gut driven by far more than just being confronted by yet another dead body. There's something familiar about this woman…

John skids to a stop beside me and then hunches down to touch the shoulder of the corpse and turn it over. I jump back with a strangled groan when the face is revealed.

It *is* her. As if my thoughts have just conjured her up.

I'm looking at Felicity, the federal agent who reached out to me all those months ago. The dead body is that of the woman who wanted me to turn against my husband and help her put him in prison.

And her throat has been well and truly cut.

Rio

144

I'M in the middle of yet another argument with Nicky about the Martelli situation when the call comes through from Danelli that a body has been found in the orchard.

I lurch up to my feet from behind my desk and release a curse when I hear who the dead person is.

"And Boss," Danelli adds. "Your wife and sister are down there too."

"*What*? Get them back to the house now! Put them down in the safe room until we know more."

Along with the shooting range, I had the safe room with an attached escape tunnel built the moment I purchased this place, but I hoped never to have to actually use it. The room sits directly beneath the entrance foyer, and the tunnel leads beneath the house and property to emerge out near the helipad.

I turn to my brother. "Nicky—"

"I know, Rio. I am not done with my objections, but we can resume that discussion another time. What do you need?"

"You're armed?"

He flashes a grin and lifts his jacket to show the holstered gun. "Always."

"Then follow me."

I've never bothered to venture into the orchard, but of course I know where it is. I've studied the plans and layout of this property in intimate detail. Even if I didn't know what direction to take on leaving the house, it would be easy to confirm by simply following the line of security men all rushing to the area.

When I reach the orchard, Danelli is already there, directing men to cordon the area off while simultaneously on a phone call to arrange for a body bag and removal team.

"Nicky, talk to Danelli. Find out what you can about the

situation and report back to me. Remind him this could be a diversion, so don't remove guards off the other entrances, or from the CCTV control room.

"I need to know who killed her, and whether she's working alone or if we're about to get a visit from a swarm of Feds. Or worse."

Nicky's face is grim, his usual humorous expression missing. "Will do, brother."

He heads over to my second, and I bring my attention back to the body. Bianca is kneeling beside it, leaning in to look at something one of the security guys hands her, while Angel hovers nearby, being gently restrained by a bodyguard and looking pale and like she's about to lose her breakfast.

"Why are my wife and sister still here?" Everyone around me jerks or recoils at my loud tone.

Everyone except Bianca, who turns to face me before gesturing me closer. "Rio, come look."

Interestingly, her cheeks may be as pale as Angel's, but she doesn't seem as if she's about to throw up. Far from it. Instead, there is speculation in her eyes as she holds out a piece of paper and waves it at me, then turns back to the corpse.

I stride forward and squat down beside her.

"No bullet wound," she says, then shudders. "Looks like her throat was cut with a knife."

She's correct. The agent's throat has been slit in a clean and professional-looking manner. One slice.

There's a pool of blood congealing around her body, which means she wasn't killed elsewhere and dumped here. She was murdered in this spot, on my land, and most likely while my family and I slept earlier this morning, judging by the rigor mortis that has started to set in to her limbs.

Bianca hands me a badge and a government agency ID card. "John found these on the body," she says. Then she adds in a whisper I'm not sure I'm meant to hear, "Poor thing."

I stare down silently at the ID. This woman, Felicity Ramirez, worked hard during the past year or two to try and bring me down. She wasn't powerful enough to succeed, but she did cause issues for my crew—and created plenty of work for my lawyer, Carnarvon.

Her demise may not fill me with sadness, but it could potentially cause all manner of problems if there is any hint that I or anyone from my organization is implicated in the death of a federal agent.

"I guess she was still trying to find some dirt on you," Bianca says quietly. "I feel sorry for her, though. She wasn't...bad. And she was always nice to me."

The bodyguard has something in his fist. When I hold out my palm and shoot him a stony look, he flinches a little. He knows my orders were to remove my wife and sister from this scene. But when he passes me a handwritten note, my annoyance with him fades as shock takes its place.

The note, scrawled in pencil, contains the address of this property and the words, *Apple orchard, M. 06:00.*

M? She was meeting someone here? Who, and why? Someone from my crew? Or someone from Martelli's crew? His men have been charged with guarding the perimeter, and some of them are stationed in nearby towns to keep track of comings and goings in the area.

If the agent came into this county on any of the main car routes, then a warning should have been received already.

Is "M" Martelli? Or is it worse than that? An internal betrayal from my team, like the nanny, Penn? Like Bianca said her mother hinted at?

I raise my head and turn to study everyone in the vicinity, looking for any hint of wrongness. It's here. I know it is. I *feel* it. And yet, the only men here are those from *my* crew.

Mitch, my wife's usual bodyguard who was off duty this morning, has obviously been recalled from his bed and is combing through the foliage beyond the body. M? He must feel my gaze on his back because he suddenly lifts his head, like a hound scenting the breeze, and turns to face me.

A quick nod in my direction, and then he returns to his duty. Nothing untoward there…but I still feel it in my gut… Something not quite right…

"Boss, the clean-up team is here. Shall I send them in?"

I turn to Danelli and give him a short nod. "Get my wife and sister out of here first. They don't need to see that."

"Right away, sir." He barks out orders, and I listen, and look, and finally remember that Danelli's first name, which I haven't used in years, is Michael.

"Patience is not simply the ability to wait – it's how we behave while we're waiting."
Joyce Meyer

Bianca

SO MANY QUESTIONS, and not a single answer is forthcoming. I'm holed up here in what the bodyguards call "the safe room," with Angel, Emilia, and the nanny, Susan, as well as John, Tony, and Santo, who've been ordered to stay with us and wait for instructions.

I pace back and forth and worry about what's happening above our heads.

The room isn't huge, but it is large enough for a seating area with a couple of armchairs and sofas, and there is what looks like a coffee station in the corner, containing a water cooler, coffee machine, and cups. There's a rack of magazines, too, and when I check the publication dates on them, my heart gives a little flip-flop. They're from this week.

Did Rio just stock the room with reading matter, expecting an imminent crisis? Or is he simply thorough to have the space tended to on a regular basis? Knowing Rio, either option could be true.

The walls look like normal painted drywall, just without any windows, of course, because we're several feet underground.

But when I ask Santo what makes this space safer than anywhere else in the house, he knocks on the wall and says, "Concrete, ma'am, and steel plating beneath the drywall. Plus, no one is getting through either of these doors in a hurry."

The door we came through is heavy—some kind of reinforced metal with a huge bolt that John shifted into place across the middle as soon as we were all inside and heading down the stairs. Santo and Tony carried the stroller down, while I clung tightly to Emilia.

The door at the other end of the rectangular room is equally bolted.

"Where does that lead?" I ask, pointing at the door.

Again, it's Santo who pipes up. "The escape tunnel. Emerges out past the house, near the helipad."

My mind boggles at the amount of money it must have taken for Rio to get this all set up. Just on the off chance that we may need to use the house one day. How many other "safe houses" does he have dotted around the country, and are all of them as well equipped as this one?

I understand Rio's need to protect us—his women—but I want to be up there, too. If something were to happen to him, we only have the tenuous ear mic communication in the bodyguards' ears to keep us informed.

Why would they kill Felicity? And who are *they*, for that

matter? She worked for the government and tried hard to bring Rio down. She almost succeeded, until I disappeared to Cleveland, and from what I was told after Rio brought me back, Carnarvon managed to put that threat to bed—presumably by paying the right people and greasing the right palms.

I can't imagine anyone on Rio's payroll doing such a thing. To kill a federal agent and leave the body on Rio's land to be found in such a random manner is asking for all sorts of trouble.

Is this the work of my birth mother or the person she said was working with her? Did Rina somehow find out where we are and tell the Feds, then get Felicity to turn up here for a meeting, only to kill her? It just doesn't make sense. And who in hell is M, if that note was referring to an actual person?

Martelli's men are here, supposedly in support of Rio. He hasn't told me why, only that it involves Nicky and that the unpleasant boss from Washington is now firmly on our side.

I don't trust that man. He made my skin crawl when we attended his daughter's engagement party a short while ago, and nothing has changed in that regard.

Is he the M in the note? I still don't understand why he or one of his men would kill a Fed? Unless it was specifically to frame Rio.

Nothing makes sense about this latest death, and the whirling thoughts in my head are frustrating me to infinity and beyond.

On some level, I know I'm using the conundrum to occupy my mind and avoid remembering the image of Felicity's open-mouthed, slack features above that gaping wound across her neck. I don't want to think about that congealing mess of squelchy blood that John exposed when he rolled her body over...

My stomach flip-flops in protest, and for a moment I worry I'm going to throw up. But I can't do that. I need to display some control. The nanny is rocking a sleeping Emilia in her stroller, but she's staring at me with fear in her eyes and giving the impression she's looking to me for a sign as to whether or not she should panic.

And Angel... My sister-in-law is curled up in an armchair over in a shadowed corner of the room. She's quietly crying, and I remember with a start that she's only nineteen.

I'm Rio's wife now, which means I can't fall apart. In his absence, people are relying on me to remain calm.

I stride over and kneel down in front of Angel. "Shh, hon, it's okay. We'll be okay. Rio is sorting out everything, and then when it's safe, he'll let us know. He will protect us, Angel. I promise."

Can I promise that? No, of course I can't. But she needs to hear positive words right now.

She raises a tear-stained face and scrubs at her cheeks as if embarrassed. "They shipped me away early on, Bianca. To keep me away from stuff like...like this. I was pretty much raised by the staff at the school in Switzerland, you know. So, I've never actually seen a..." She swallows convulsively before finishing. "A dead body, before today."

I almost laugh but just manage to rein in the totally inappropriate response. The only dead bodies I'd ever seen before her brother kidnapped me off the street were those animals in the shelter who weren't lucky enough to make it. I didn't even view my mother's body after the car accident. My father wouldn't let me, said it would be too traumatic.

And now I'm a killer, with blood on my own hands, and I'm comforting the sister of a person who is essentially a mob boss and murderer. My husband. Whom I love with all my heart.

"Try not to think about it at the moment, hon." I rub her thigh gently, wondering whether the advice I'm giving is really for her or for me. I squeeze her knee. "It was pretty horrible, I know, and we can talk about it all later because that's better than holding it in, but for now, let's just focus on staying calm and knowing that Rio will look after us. We'll be out of here in no time."

I hope.

I shoot a glance at the goons, who are standing in a group near the stairs that lead down here. The door to the safe room is hidden behind a tapestry wall hanging just inside the entrance of the guest wing, and until they shifted the tapestry and revealed the door, I never knew it was there.

All three men are unsmiling. They look as if their faces have been carved from granite.

I raise an inquiring brow, querying without words whether there's any news from above, but John shakes his head. No word yet.

I turn back to Angel and keep patting her knee. "Tell me more about Switzerland and the school you went to, Angel. My dad lives in Thailand now, somewhere in the mountains, but I've never been overseas. Is it very different in Switzerland? Better than here? What did you like about it? Have you traveled other places too? Where's your favorite?"

She takes a deep inhale and lets it out slowly, and while there's still a hitch in her breathing, I'm pleased that she manages to launch into a description of the place she spent most of her formative years.

I half listen, murmuring responses at appropriate points in the conversation, but the bulk of my attention remains focused on John. When he suddenly lifts his head and raises a hand to his ear, I launch up to my feet.

"Yes? What is it?"

He's clearly just received some kind of message.

"I'm sorry, ma'am," he says, and then points to the sofa near where I'm standing. "You should take a seat. Boss said we'll need to stay down here a while longer. He said law enforcement has just arrived up top."

"Law enforcement?" Does he mean local police? Or…

"Feds, ma'am. Apparently, they've come in force. With warrants."

21

"Beware of false knowledge; it is more dangerous than ignorance."
George Bernard Shaw

Rio

"I NEED YOU HERE NOW, CARNARVON," I bark into the phone, rage roiling in my chest like molten lava.

Now I'm certain this is an inside job. Someone lured a federal agent to my property and then killed her. And then sat back to watch the carnage unfold.

Agents are swarming the house and grounds, but they're too late to find their colleague. My clean-up crew has come and gone. And my clean-up crew is the best in the business.

They will probably find the safe-room entrance soon, or the exit from the safe room at the end of the long tunnel I had built if they're combing the grounds that thoroughly. I want my lawyer here before that. Because neither the entrance nor the exit to the safe space is possible to breach from the outside.

And I will not allow them in to harass my wife. The more I can keep Bianca, as well as my sister and daughter, out of this mess, the better for them all.

"I'm already en route, sir," my lawyer answers. "Coming in by helicopter."

I remove the phone from my ear and stare at it in shock before putting it back. Who gave Carnarvon permission to fly here, without informing me first? "Why?"

"I have some matters to discuss relating to your Mediterranean businesses. Tommaso reported in last night and disclosed some information that is best discussed in person. No trail, so to speak. I alerted your second earlier today to arrange a time, and he okayed the visit."

Danelli. Again. "How long until you arrive?"

"Ten minutes, perhaps?"

"I'll meet you at the helipad."

"No need. I am familiar with your current location, if you recall."

Indeed, Carnarvon was instrumental in purchasing this place and gaining approval from local authorities for the various modifications I've since had installed.

"May I suggest you remain in the house," he adds, "and ensure no papers are removed from your office before I get there. I have every confidence we will get this situation sorted quickly, sir."

His suggestion makes sense. I have the relevant permits—thanks to Carnarvon—for the indoor shooting range and every firearm in this place for myself and every member of my crew. Martelli's men have been assisting only peripherally, manning the perimeter and doing some of the lesser fetch-and-carry tasks that have freed up my crew to be here on the ground.

Quite frankly, if one of Martelli's crew is carrying without a firearms permit, that is not my issue. It will be his.

Some of the papers in my office, on the other hand, while not incriminating, could be sensitive to current business operations and negotiations, and I would prefer they remain private and out of federal agency hands.

Quickly, I end the call and do as Carnarvon suggests, striding into my office, where I find two agents already flicking through papers on my desk.

I relax slightly. They haven't yet discovered the safe that sits behind the drinks trolley near the bookcase.

I stroll over to the trolley and make a show of pouring myself a whiskey. It is after noon, and it has already been one hell of a week.

"Want one?" I lift my glass and take a sip.

Both agents shake their heads.

The older one, who seems to be in charge judging by the way the other one keeps looking to him for direction, points to the locked wooden cabinet that sits behind my desk, between two of the floor-to-ceiling windows.

"Not while on duty," he says in a bored tone, as if used to propositions from organized crime bosses. "I need this opened."

"I was only offering a whiskey. Not a bribe." I smile at them and sip some more.

His eyes narrow. "Where's the key?"

I place the glass down on the trolley and cross my arms over my chest, letting my annoyance show through. "I was

157

advised by one of your colleagues outside in the gardens that you are here because you suspect I have killed one of your own. Let me assure you, I have *not*."

I allow the truth of that last statement to ring through in the words, and the older agent straightens from looking at the cabinet and studies me. His head tips slightly to one side, as if he hasn't considered the possibility of my innocence until this moment.

"Innocence" being a relative term, of course. I have done many things, and I am about as far from innocent as one can get without being the actual devil himself. But I did not kill their agent, and therefore in that fact alone, I can truthfully proclaim my innocence.

"You will find files in that cabinet, not a dead body."

The agent glares at me, the momentary doubt about my guilt dissipating. "Key?" he barks and holds out a hand.

I grin. "It is kept upstairs in my bedside table."

"Then lead the way."

"Follow me, gentlemen."

How far away is Carnarvon? How long do I have to keep stringing this out in such a farcical manner? I stroll from the office and take my time leading them upstairs.

Even if my lawyer does get here in the next few minutes, what will he be able to do in this situation? He has standing permission to do whatever it takes to protect the Agosti family and organization.

But here, where a dead agent was killed and now a tip-off to the agency in question has been provided—an obvious one given how many agents swarmed to the apple orchard instead of the house—how far will my lawyer need to go to "sort" the situation, as he put it in our phone conversation?"

I hear the incoming helicopter at the same time as the two agents accompanying me upstairs. I pause with my hand on the bedroom door handle while they stop in the hallway and stare at each other, clearly wondering who is about to join their party.

"My lawyer is about to arrive, I believe."

"Fuck," the younger agent mutters, then snaps his mouth shut as if he didn't mean to let that slip.

"Oh, I forgot, gentlemen," I say. "The key isn't up here after all. I just remembered that I keep it downstairs in a drawer in my desk."

They turn and thunder back down the staircase, and then the older agent stops the other one with a hand to the arm. They stand at the base of the stairs and mutter to each other.

As I follow them down at a more sedate pace, their voices float upward. They are debating whether to check out the helicopter or continue their search. They decide on the latter, heading back into the office.

I stroll in to see them trying every drawer. "Here," I offer, leaning forward and removing the tiny key from where it resides beneath a set of pens that sit in a solid-based holder atop the desk.

The taller of the two agents grabs the key from my fingers and shoves it into the cabinet. When they pull it open, the drawers are empty. I've only just had the cabinet installed and not had the time to fill it.

"What the fuck?" The older agent glares into the empty top drawer then up at me. "I should arrest you for wasting our time."

"You may try, if you wish." I try to keep my tone gentle, but the younger man takes an involuntary step backward.

Must be something in the way I study him? As if I would like to remove him from the face of the earth. "Depends if you want to keep your job."

"Threats, too, Agosti? Right, I've had enough of this. You—"

"Gentlemen." Carnarvon bustles into the room, then stops and studies us all. He pushes his spectacles higher on his nose and stares at the older agent, who he has obviously clocked within seconds is the more senior of these two.

I admit to myself that I'm rather pleased to see him.

"My client has done nothing wrong," he continues in his scratchy yet effective voice. "You have agents combing the grounds as well as this home, from what I've seen already, but you have found nothing, I assume? Because, of course, there is nothing to find. What is the basis for this continued intrusion of my client's privacy? To whom should we direct our complaint and our claim for compensation?"

"Your what? You…you…"

"It is not rocket science, gentlemen. Who is in charge of this operation today? I plan to make a complaint on behalf of my client, Gregorio Agosti, and I require the details of whomever is in charge. Is it you? I will need your badge and ID, thank you." He points a finger at the shorter agent.

As predicted, he quickly shakes his head.

When the lawyer turns his gaze on the other agent, still standing by the empty cabinet, the man shrugs. "Neither of us is in charge, as you likely well know. We've been given instructions to search this room. Agent Jamie Frederick is in charge today. You'll find him outside in the orchard, I believe."

Carnarvon's brows rise, and I can't quite hold in my smirk. He is doing very well today. "The orchard? What a strange place for an investigation. Gentlemen, you had best hasten your search because it will be halted in less than five minutes."

Carnarvon turns away, lifting his phone and dialing, and gives me a surreptitious wink as he strides out of the room. I privately vow to raise his retainer from tomorrow onward.

True to his word, whatever calls Carnarvon makes and whoever he speaks with proves effective. The word spreads among the agents combing the house, and slowly, they all traipse out to congregate in a disgruntled group on the driveway near the front of the house. I stand in the doorway at the front entrance and watch as those on the grounds also make their way over to join the group.

A tall balding guy with rimless spectacles waves his hand for attention. Agent Frederick, I presume.

"Fall out, guys," he announces. "False alarm, it seems."

His tone is both annoyed and resigned.

Mutterings among the team ensue, and several of them shoot angry glances my way. They can hate me all they wish; I truly do not care. As long as they leave my property, and leave my family and businesses in peace, then they can glare all they like.

I did not kill their agent, though I'm damn sure going to find out who did. And then I may just send the information about the killer as a gift to Agent Frederick.

"Who in the hell did you call?" I ask my lawyer as he joins me in the doorway.

We watch as the army of agents pile into their vehicles and begin to leave in the same slow convoy-style in which they first arrived.

"Best not to ask," he mutters, but when I turn and spear him with an inquiring look, he adds, "Apologies, sir. I forgot you prefer to be apprised of all details. Many of my clients do not. I'll have a list of names sent to you by morning. A mix of bribes and blackmail. Works wonders."

"Send it to me tonight," I say, asserting my authority in as subtle a manner as I can, given how well he performed today.

He nods with a respectful air.

"Now," I add as Nicky rounds a corner of the building and stares after the departing vehicles. "Give me ten minutes to sort a few loose ends out here, and then I will meet you inside for our discussion.

"Perhaps the rear sitting room rather than my office. I don't fancy trying to sort through the mess of papers they left on my desk just yet."

The sitting room, located at the rear of the main house on the first floor, is smaller and more private than the large main living area. It will be suitable for whatever discussion needs to take place.

Which reminds me—why did Danelli not let me know that Carnarvon was on his way here?

"Feel free to ask the housekeeper on your way through to arrange a drink, Carnarvon. Or something to eat. I assume you'll stay over tonight? You did very well in there."

"Thank you, sir." He melts away inside, and I step down to speak with Nicky and give orders for the guards to be doubled until further notice.

I also ask him to keep a close eye on Danelli.

He shoots me a puzzled look. "Why? I mean, yeah, sure, I will, but why?"

The admission practically sticks in my throat, and I have to force the words past my lips. "Someone tried to set me up, Nicky. Someone who knows this place, knows there's a mostly hidden apple orchard located on the premises, and knew enough about the agent Felicity and her previous dealings with me to lure her here—no doubt with promises of helping to bring me down. The Feds went straight to the orchard when they arrived."

"I did notice that, but then I got caught up in the clean-up, so it didn't occur to me to wonder. It is likely to be an inside job, then? I heard about the note, and the mysterious M. I was trying to figure out how it might relate to Rina Carlotti, but her involvement in this didn't make sense."

"Indeed, it does not on the surface. I do not know how it ties in with Bianca's mother, or if, indeed, it does tie in with her at all. But I am not a huge believer in coincidence. It is all linked somehow. I feel the truth of that in here." I fist my hand and tap my chest.

It galls me that I cannot simply look at each of my men and discern which of them is a double-crossing traitor. It isn't enough to sense that it's one of mine. I should be able to sense *who*. The fact that I cannot pinpoint the individual suggests it is likely someone I have learned to trust. And perhaps that trust is blinding me.

"Maybe it's Martelli?" Nicky's tone is hopeful.

"Or Mitch. Or any of the other members of my crew whose names begin with M. There are several."

He frowns. "So why do you want me to watch Danelli, then, if—"

"First name, Michael."

"Ah." Nicky whistles, and I lift my hand and rub my temple.

A headache is forming, and I can't afford the distraction. "Of course, it may not be him, but I am possibly too close to see it. He has been at my side for many years. Keep an eye on the man and let me know if you notice anything untoward. Anything, Nicky."

"I will." He releases a small sigh and then a self-deprecating laugh. "For my sake, I hope M *is* that bastard Martelli. The last thing I ever want to do is marry his murderous daughter."

22

"Violence, even well-intentioned, always rebounds upon oneself."
Lao Tzu

Bianca

WHEN WE FINALLY EMERGE FROM the safe room, Rio meets us just outside the door. I run into his embrace and wrap my arms tightly around his middle, breathing in his scent to try and calm my over-stimulated system.

I know rationally there must have been air flow down there—though how the quality remained decent was one thing I didn't ask the goons to explain. But it felt so claustrophobic and cloying that it was like we were all about to suffocate. It's so good to be free. And to have Rio's warm strength wrapped around me, even if just for a minute or two.

I hope we never have to go down there again.

Angel is pale and quiet, which is unlike her, and Susan wipes tears surreptitiously on Emilia's blanket as she emerges with my daughter in her arms. We all stand and watch as Tony and Santo maneuver Emilia's stroller up the stairs and out into the house.

"Are you all right?" I ask Rio in a quiet tone. I still don't want to alarm Angel, but I have to know what happened. "It was difficult down there, not knowing what was going on."

Rio places a kiss on my forehead and pushes locks of my hair back over my shoulders. I should probably start plaiting it. Or get it cut. It always seems to be in the way.

I don't know why I'm thinking about my hair. Maybe because that's easier than dealing with the reality that death has once again come to our door. Literally.

Rio's touch is gentle, as if he can sense my distress, and I lean into him.

"Everything is fine," he says. "My lawyer worked a minor miracle to send away a whole platoon of Feds from the estate. They'd obviously been tipped off about the dead agent, but my crew worked too fast and too efficiently for them to find anything incriminating."

How is that possible? I frown and open my mouth to speak, but he raises a hand.

"Trust me on that. There was nothing for them to find, Bianca."

What did his crew do with poor Felicity? Will her family be left wondering forevermore where she is?

"Um, Rio. Will you let her loved ones know somehow?"

Rio draws back and studies me with a perplexed frown. "I... Why?"

"Please? Imagine how you'd feel if I simply disappeared forever, seemingly off the face of the earth. I know you didn't kill her, but at least give them the opportunity to have some closure."

"I guess I could arrange that." He sounds nonplussed, as if my request is something he's never considered before.

"Thank you." It's all I can offer the agent, and of course it's not enough.

I try to shut down the little voice in my head that keeps whispering, *Is this to do with Rina? Is this somehow all the fault of the Carlottis and our crazy, tainted bloodline?*

Rio is still talking, using a soothing tone as if he senses I'm on the edge of losing it. He sounds like I did when I was talking to Angel earlier, and I stifle a totally inappropriate laugh.

"…Carnarvon worked a kind of magic behind the scenes to call the Feds off from their hunt. I intend to give him a raise from tomorrow onward."

My limbs fill with a sudden strange lethargy. Was I being held up before by adrenaline? Has it suddenly worn off? I feel like I'm about to collapse from relief. "Sounds like he earned the raise."

Angel clears her throat. She's wandered close and has heard part of our conversation.

"Bianca was amazing down there," she says. "She kept me calm, Rio. She made me talk about school and travel to stop me from freaking out, even though I know she was probably just as scared as me."

Rio places a finger beneath my chin and tilts it up. There is pride in his eyes, and love. I hope he can see the same thing reflected back at him.

"Bianca *is* amazing," he says, then leans in and kisses me on the lips.

Surprisingly, he tastes of whiskey, and I dart out my tongue and lick him, only just restraining myself from groaning with pleasure.

I love the taste of my husband. Whiskey-laced or otherwise. Now is not the place for exploring that, of course, but I decide to tease him just a little.

"We were stuck down there while you were up here drinking, husband?"

I know that whatever went on up here was likely less pleasant than what we were dealing with in the safe room. All we had to do was sit and wait.

He laughs lightly. "It is almost dinner time, little bird. Whiskey is more than appropriate."

My eyes widen. "We were down there that long? No wonder my stomach is growling."

In truth, the thought of eating anything at present makes me feel ill, but I can't deny that my stomach is protesting its emptiness.

Rio smiles and taps the tip of my nose. "I will join you later. But for now, I must head in to meet with Carnarvon. We will be in the small sitting room if you need me for anything."

Then he leans in and whispers in my ear in a voice so quiet I know only I can hear the words. "I am incredibly proud of you, Bianca. I love you."

I squeeze my arms tightly for a moment around his waist, then release him. "Don't be too late with your business meeting. A wife has needs, you know."

Angel suddenly makes a gagging noise, and the small circle of awareness that had shrunk to include just Rio and me expands once again to include everyone here. My cheeks burn with heat at the sight of the nanny and all three goons studiously making every effort to look away from us.

Angel mimes putting her fingers down her throat, and I laugh and step away from Rio.

"Come on." I link my arm through Angel's and gesture to

Susan to join us with my daughter. "Girl power. Let's go upstairs and have a little feast of celebration together in Emilia's suite. It's been a pretty shit day, and we made it through okay. I think we all deserve some time out."

When I glance over my shoulder, I catch a glimpse of Rio's face as he turns away from us. The indulgent smile he sent our way disappears as if it never existed at all, and a grim focus takes its place.

I don't think he's aware I'm watching him. He straightens his shoulders and strides down the hallway away from us, the line of his body holding tension and his hands clenched into fists by his sides.

In a split second of hyper-awareness, I remember that our problems have not gone away.

They may have been "sorted" this afternoon by a clever lawyer and a crew who knows how to hide evidence of a crime, but the threat to our family's safety and happiness still remains.

And in that split-second moment, sadness almost consumes me. I falter, missing my footing on the first step and almost tripping over my own feet before Angel and Susan right me and we continue up the stairs.

But the truth about my future with Rio is once again clear in my mind. The threat of violence and death will always be present, as long as I remain married to a mob boss.

23

"The world breaks everyone, and afterward, some are strong at the broken places."
Ernest Hemingway

Bianca

DUSK HAS COME AND GONE, and night is settling in when I leave Emilia's room intending to head downstairs to look for Rio.

My daughter is finally asleep, the nanny watching over her, and Angel has just retired to her room after giving me a huge hug and a subdued thank you for helping her today.

Mrs. Jarvis sent up trays of food and drinks for us, including two different types of delicious-looking home-made pizzas as well as the obligatory bowl of pureed vegetables and a bottle of milk for Emilia.

But I couldn't bring myself to eat more than a couple of mouthfuls. I kept thinking about the agent, Felicity, and how alive she was last time I saw her on that tourist walk in

Boston. I can barely equate that memory with the mutilated and bloody corpse I saw this morning.

She didn't deserve that.

For me to sit and pretend happy families, reading Emilia a bedtime story while listening to Susan and Angel chat quietly in the background, seemed ludicrously wrong. I noticed when the trays were collected after dinner that the pizzas were barely touched. Seems none of us had much of an appetite for food.

The house is quiet, but everywhere I look, goons lurk in the shadows. Rio has clearly stepped up the security. Several of them trail me down the stairs, and I shoot a look over my shoulder and shake my head when I see my usual bodyguard, Mitch, is one of them.

"Mitch! When did you last sleep?"

He frowns. "Early this morning, ma'am. I'm fine."

"Well, do you know what? So am I. I can barely move without tripping over one of you. Please, I'm just going downstairs to say good night to Rio and then grab a small snack from the kitchen. And then I'll be back up here to tuck myself safely into bed. That's it, I promise."

"But, ma'am—"

"Go stand guard again outside my daughter's suite. Please." I look beyond him at the other three standing awkwardly on the stairs. "All of you. There are more guards downstairs, I presume?"

The goon behind Mitch nods with a reluctant air, and I spread my hands out.

"So, I'm good. Go back to your post. Guard my daughter."

Thank God they listen to me in the end. This is overkill,

and if it stays like this, a goon every ten feet or so, we'll all end up stark-raving mad after a few days.

I wander through the house toward the small sitting room at the rear where Rio said he'd be meeting with Carnarvon. That was a while ago now, but I can still hear the low murmur of voices on the other side of the door.

I knock and poke my head into the room at Rio's terse command to enter. Papers are spread out on the coffee table between him and his lawyer. A three-quarters-empty coffee pot sits on the table beside two used cups, and a plate of sugared cookies sits seemingly untouched and pushed off to one side.

Rio is in shirtsleeves, minus his tie, and his usually immaculate hair is a little roughed up, as if he's rubbed his hand through it one too many times. He looks tired and fed up.

Carnarvon, on the other hand, looks as prim and proper as ever, still in a suit jacket and tie, and with his spectacles perched high on his nose.

"I'm heading to bed soon, Rio. Will you be much longer here?"

He rubs the back of his neck and turns his head one way and then the other, stretching his muscles. "We'll be done here soon, Bianca."

"Okay." I nod toward the lawyer. "Good night. I guess we'll see you at breakfast."

"Good night, Mrs. Agosti. Yes, see you then."

I scoot in and swipe a cookie off the plate with a quick grin at Rio before leaving them to it. I head to the kitchen, planning to grab a glass of milk. I'm still not hungry, but I need to eat something to keep up my strength. Cookies and milk are something my delicate stomach will likely tolerate.

The kitchen is empty, the counters clean. Mrs. Jarvis must have retired for the night. There is one light still on over the central counter above the cooktop, and a square of light spills out from the butler's pantry. The rest of the room is in darkness.

I sink down onto one of the chairs at the table and take a bite of my cookie before running the fingers of my other hand over the smooth wooden dining surface.

The last time I sat here with Rio and his family feels like forever ago. I was filled with hope for the future at that dinner, determined to bring a slice of "normal" into Rio's life.

It may have been only a few days ago, but right now, hope for the future is much more difficult to sustain in my heart. I just feel tired, as if I don't have the energy to keep running from whatever threat is likely to be thrown in our path next.

I finish my cookie and lean my head down on the table surface, closing my eyes and just enjoying the solitude for a minute or two. Thinking about the past. Was it really less than two years ago that I was still Bree Walker, working in animal rescue and planning to down an espresso martini with Dave and Shelley for my twenty-fifth birthday?

I laugh slightly and lift my head before opening my eyes and letting out a sigh.

Never in a million years would I have imagined back then that my life would lead to this.

But I love Rio and my daughter more than anything, and I am going to have to figure out a way to survive in this cutthroat world, moving forward. Because I don't want to leave him. Not anymore. It would be like cutting out half of my own heart to do such a thing now.

A tiny sound from the butler's pantry draws my attention,

and I stifle a groan before climbing to my feet. My solitude was far too short-lived. Is it a goon, down here like me to snatch a quick bite of something before heading back to their station, or is it the cook finishing off her work for the night?

"Mrs. Jarvis?" I call out and start toward the pantry, but there's no answer.

Only an ominous silence.

My heart begins to speed up while, conversely, my feet slow down. I come to a stop, studying the square of light beaming from the doorway and wondering if I imagined the sound.

"Hello?"

Nothing.

Okay. This isn't good. I begin to back away as quietly as I can, but I only manage a few feet before I bump into the edge of the central counter. And at that moment, a shadowy form appears in the doorway before stepping out to show her face.

Smiling at me as if my appearance has made her day.

Not a goon. Not by any stretch of the imagination. And definitely not Mrs. Jarvis.

Rina Carlotti stands there in my kitchen, grinning at me, and in her right hand, she wields the largest chef's knife I've ever seen.

"A false friend and a shadow attend only when the sun shines."
Benjamin Franklin

Rio

I'VE SPENT the best part of two hours talking with Carnarvon through a range of issues that have arisen recently in my businesses based in Catania. The housekeeper brought us dinner and drinks on trays earlier, and we ended up eating while we worked.

Carnarvon alerted me to some new trade restrictions that may impact the flow of product through the local port, and we've looked at a number of options for how to get around that.

The businesses there are largely legitimate, though, and there has been nothing in the discussion so far that couldn't have been addressed by phone or email.

As he tries to hand me yet another contract to sign, there's a knock at the door.

"Come," I call out, wondering if the housekeeper is back to clear out the trays.

Bianca leans her head in, asking how much longer we'll be.

My headache is worse than it was earlier, and my neck and shoulders ache from bending over this infernal coffee table.

I rub the back of my neck and stretch it out, trying to ease the cricks. "We'll be done here soon, Bianca."

"Okay." She wishes Carnarvon good night and then scampers in to swipe a cookie off the tray.

Cheeky little minx. My cock stirs as she shoots me a grin, but I tamp down the desire, promising myself we will have time together later. Now, I need to find out what Carnarvon really wants.

I lean back on the sofa in a semblance of relaxation. "Tell me," I say in a conversational tone. "Why are you here, Carnarvon? What is it that couldn't be said over the phone?"

"Ah." He leans back too, dropping the contract in his hand onto the coffee table between us and removing his spectacles to rub his eyes. When he places them back on his nose, he releases a small sigh. "I've been trying to work out how to tell you this, but there's no easy way, so I'm just going to come straight out and say it. Your second, Michael Danelli, has been making some strange decisions of late, so I took the liberty of looking into his behavior."

My pulse jumps, but I sit still, not wanting to show my lawyer that his revelation disturbs me. I still don't know for sure if Danelli is the traitor, but it is sounding more likely by the minute.

"And what have you found?"

"I've found a number of anomalies, sir. I am sorry to be the one to bring this to your attention, but I think your second may be feeding information to someone outside the Agosti organization."

"I see." Silence falls in the room as I process his words.

The more I consider it, the more it makes sense. Someone on the inside is working for my enemy. And yet...

I tune in to my instinct, and I can't see it. I genuinely can't see it. Not Danelli.

I have no real friends, never have or likely will in this world. But Danelli has always been the closest thing to a friend I will ever get in this life. Something in my gut tells me Danelli isn't our resident rat.

But then, who is? And now, with Carnarvon's revelation, how can I ignore the possibility that I'm wrong?

Have I steered my family *toward* danger all this time, rather than protected them from it?

"I need more, Carnarvon. I need evidence to back up that statement. Do you have any?"

"Unfortunately, I do, sir." He sits forward and shuffles some of the papers on the desk, then makes a *tsk* noise between his teeth and turns instead to the briefcase sitting on the sofa beside him. "I knew you would require proof, and I've brought it with me. I am sorry, sir. Very sorry about this."

I grunt noncommittally, and while I wait for him to produce his evidence, my gaze falls to the mess of papers already on the table. The contract he wanted me to sign sits on top. My eye catches the logo at the base of the page.

M. C. Carnarvon & Son.

I still, though my thoughts speed up to what feels like warp level. Carnarvon's first name is Miguel. I've spent so many years referring to him by his last name that I didn't remember that fact until this very moment.

My inner monster rears its head, growling softly deep down inside. I rest one ankle across my knee, the action bringing my ankle holster close to my waiting hands.

"Tell me, Miguel." I keep my tone pseudo-friendly, but the moment I use his first name, Carnarvon freezes. "How long have you been on Rina Carlotti's payroll?"

He stops shuffling through papers and slowly turns to face me, paling when he sees the gun I've quietly slipped into my hand and pointed right at his chest.

"I won't miss from this distance. And we won't even be interrupted. I have the silencer on, see?" I tap the piece at the end of the gun. "You have ten seconds to tell me the truth, Miguel."

"Rio, please…"

"Nine seconds. No, now it's eight."

"Wait. I…"

"Seven."

"Yes, it's true. But don't shoot me, please. It's my son, sir. My son's life that hangs in the balance. I have to protect him. You know what that's like. Please…" He waves his hands frantically, looking as if he's about to bring up his dinner.

"How long?" I ask again.

"Since you found the missing Carlotti girl," he admits, and I blink a couple of times, not having expected the deception to have extended for that long.

"Rossi approached me not long after you kidnapped her. Said he had a plan in motion to bring you down, and that if it succeeded, I would be brought in on retainer and would have more money than I would know what to do with for the rest of my life."

My finger spasms on the trigger, and Carnarvon's eyes dart down and back up to my face.

"I said no!" He practically shouts the words before he slumps back in the chair. It's the first time I've ever seen the man flustered. "Truly, I did say no."

"But you said yes eventually."

"I did," he admits, "but not until they threatened Rico. My son. Not directly, of course, but they set him up, got video and photos of him in some extremely compromising situations. Said they'd release it across worldwide media channels as well as on social media. The boy would be ruined, Rio. I had no choice. Believe me, what they had on him was…"

Carnarvon shudders. "It was very bad."

The lawyer arranges much of my dirty work. Whatever they have on his son must be extreme.

I understand his motivation, but the reality is his actions put *my* family in danger. And that is something I cannot forgive. Carnarvon knows the consequences for that as well as I do. But it seems he's still prepared to try and beg for his life.

"I'll do anything, sir, anything, please—"

"Where is Rina Carlotti?"

He opens and closes his mouth a couple of times, then slides off the sofa and down onto his knees on the floor. His hands come up in a prayer position, and he stares at me with terror in his expression.

"Where?"

There's a sick feeling in my gut that tells me to move.

"*Where*?" I roar the question at him, jumping to my feet and standing over him, and he flinches.

"She's here. I'm sorry, sir. She came in with me on the helicopter today. I let her into the house earlier before our meeting. I don't know where she is now, but I suspect she's going to go after—"

Pop, pop, pop.

Carnarvon is no more.

I haven't time to deal with the mess or process the loss of someone I trusted implicitly. I race out the door, yelling as I go for security to fall in and follow me. I'm heading for the stairs when an ear-piercing scream erupts from the direction of the kitchen.

My heart almost stops when I recognize the voice as Bianca's. I pivot, running as fast as I can in that direction. But the scream continues, on and on.

25

"As soon as you trust yourself, you will know how to live."
Johann Wolfgang von Goethe

Bianca

"HELLO, dear daughter. Fancy meeting you here this evening. You see, this time I speak in English, not Italian, because I now know that dearest Carlos was telling the truth all this time. You have forsaken your blood. *La famiglia*. You *spat* on our family and our heritage. And for that sin, dear *daughter*, you are going to die."

"Rina." My voice comes out breathless as shock squeezes my vocal cords and threatens to freeze the blood in my veins.

How in the hell did she get in here unseen?

There are goons fucking *everywhere*. Except here, obviously, right where I need one.

I can't take my eyes off the knife. Is it one of ours, nabbed from the pantry, or did she bring it with her?

What does it even matter where it came from?

The real question I should be asking myself is how in all that is holy am I going to get out of here alive?

I bring a hand up to rest on my chest. *Breathe. And think.* Whatever I'm feeling, I can't show her any sign of weakness. She will thrive on it.

She laughs and waves the knife around. The light from the central counter glints off the enormous silver blade.

"I see you are fascinated by this thing," she says. "I could not resist its allure, either, when I saw it lying in there in its special case."

She jerks her head back toward the butler's pantry and then grimaces. "Always the best for your husband, of course. His enormous power base. His effective reach. His *wife* a Carlotti princess, no less. Even his damn knives. Only Rio Agosti would have a Damascus steel Nesmuk blade in his kitchen. Do you know how much this is worth, my dear child? Eighty thousand dollars, give or take."

She's talking gibberish. She must be. Knives don't cost that much.

"That's a lot," I murmur, madly trying to figure out what to say to distract her.

If I scream and run, will she reach me before any goons get here? Where the hell are they?

She takes a couple steps toward me, and I lurch back, scuttling around the counter to place it between us. Only thing is, she rushes too, and somehow, I have now put the counter between me and the exit.

Rina is blocking the way out.

Fuck it. I suck in a breath to scream, and she quickly raises the knife, adjusting her grip on the handle.

"I wouldn't if I were you, dear. I am very, very good at knife-throwing. Possibly more adept than my stabbing skills. Did you know that knives are my weapon of choice?"

"I… No. I didn't know that."

"I have loved knives since I was a little girl. My father taught me how to use them. I'd have happily used one on Stefano the day I killed him. I wanted to slit his stupid, adulterous throat, but Carlos wouldn't let me. He said that would be too obvious. He made me use the explosive device instead so people wouldn't know it was me."

Who knew Carlos Rossi would end up being the normal one in their relationship?

I can barely take my eyes off her as she talks, but I have to find something to use as a weapon…

I risk a glance around, but the countertops are as clean as a whistle, thanks to Mrs. Jarvis and her immaculate housekeeping. There is nothing here for me to use except my wits and my bare hands.

My bare hands are useless and untrained in any sort of fighting skill. And my wits are currently failing me because of the dread stopping my thoughts on a single repeating loop.

Today is the day I die… or my mother dies at my hand. Neither option is acceptable, and yet the outcome feels inevitable.

"Guns…pfft." She turns her head and spits on the floor beside her, and I use the couple of seconds' grace to check beneath the counter.

The shelf beneath is open and contains only a couple of glass vases.

But her attention is back on me once again. "Guns are for the men. Stupid men. Always shooting each other with their phallic-symbol weapons to prove how virile and enormous their penises are."

I blink and swallow hard as the crazy urge to laugh rises up in me. My God, what is wrong with me? Why do I always want to laugh at the most inappropriate moments?

"They should just all go out and buy sports cars," she adds.

"That…um…is an interesting observation, Mother." Maybe I can channel a little bit of Nicky here. He uses "brother" whenever he wants Rio on his side.

Can I reach one of those vases and throw it at her? I step back a tiny bit, positioning myself better to grab it as soon as an opportunity arises.

"But knives…" she continues, ignoring my movement and bringing the blade up to her face to stroke her own cheek. "They are so very up close and personal, do you not think, Bianca?"

"I hadn't…err…given it a lot of thought, but you're right, of course. Very personal. Um, how did you find our location, Mother?"

It guts me to call her that, but if it causes her to hesitate even for a few seconds before she throws that knife and pierces my heart…or lunges with it and slits my throat…

Like she presumably did to Felicity Ramirez.

"Did you kill the federal agent, Mother?"

"There is no need to keep calling me that, dear. And no, my dear friend Miguel arranged that one to distract your husband from my entrance in the helicopter. A diversion, one that had a chance of causing trouble for Agosti if the federal agents had done their job properly, but no matter. That was not the true motivation."

Miguel. Who the fuck is Miguel? Which of Rio's crew is named Miguel? I know a lot of their names now, but not all. *Fuck.* I have to let Rio know.

Then what she said penetrates. "Wait. You came in…on the helicopter? But…Carnarvon came in that way."

"He did. With me. Lovely Miguel Carnarvon, who was so open to being blackmailed, thanks to that useless and twisted son of his."

Oh my God. Rio is in the other room with Carnarvon right now. Nausea churns in my belly. Somehow, I have to get out of this kitchen alive. So I can warn him. I bend my knees slightly, readying to lunge for the vase.

"Mother, I—"

"Stop. Calling. Me. That." Her eyes flash sudden rage, and I flinch back a little. "Yes, technically I gave birth to you, and I was so happy when Agosti found you—the long-lost Mafia princess. I thought there was a chance we could be a family once again.

"But we both know you have now renounced your right to call yourself a Carlotti. You are an Agosti, through and through, and as such, it is time for you to die."

I lunge for the nearest vase and launch it across the counter in a baseball-style move. The heavy base hits Rina's cheek, and she yelps.

I turn to scream for help, but instead, my legs buckle unexpectedly. I collapse to the ground, staring down at my body in disbelief and shock.

Turns out she was faster than me.

The knife handle sticks out of my upper arm, just above my elbow. The pointy end pokes out the other side. She got me. The blade has gone right through my arm.

Shock paralyzes me for a second, and then I'm moving, rolling onto my knees and using my good hand to push myself back up to my feet. I can't feel anything in the stabbed arm. It's numb, and on some level of my awareness, I figure

185

that's a good thing because I'm certain it's going to hurt like a motherfucker later.

Rina is watching me as I rise, holding her cheek, and I stare at her warily, wondering if she has another hidden weapon someplace on her body.

"Damn," she whispers, mostly to herself. "I missed."

My brain kicks into gear, and I open my mouth to yell for help. No need to worry about the big knife now.

I have it. In my body.

I release an ear-piercing scream, and I keep the sound going, not stopping even when Rina turns and starts to run for the far exit in the opposite corner of the room. She wobbles a little, as if the blow to her face affected her balance, but she's almost at the door that leads out into the staff accommodation area, which is a veritable rabbit warren of places to hide.

No, bitch. Not so fast.

Vaguely, I'm aware of roars and yells behind me and the sound of thudding footsteps. The goons are coming. Too late.

I can't wait for them, or to think, beyond knowing I have to stop her. I simply take hold of the knife handle, pull it out of my arm, and throw it at my fleeing mother's back. Against all odds, it hits near her right shoulder blade. She falters and then drops to the floor.

I stagger over to her prone body, ignoring the blood that started to gush out of my wound when I removed the weapon. *Deal with it later.*

I drop to my knees beside Rina and grab the knife with my good hand. When I pull, she grunts, but it slides out far more easily than I expect. Score one for expensive knives.

She rolls, clutching her shoulder, and I see the bloom of blood growing on the front of her white shirt beneath her hand.

She should have worn black, I think, wondering if I'm losing my mind. *Better for mob life.*

My blood drips down, mingling with hers as we both breathe heavily in a temporary stalemate. Carlotti blood, mixing together. Mine is hers, and hers now contains mine.

I place a knee on her stomach to hold her in place, but she's bleeding as much as I am and I'm guessing she doesn't have much strength to attempt moving just yet. I start to laugh, even as my vision begins to gray around the edges. "Turns out I'm a natural with a knife, too."

And now—of all times, why now?—my arm begins to burn.

"I should have put you in the car with your father," she whispers harshly. "And watched you both burn together. You're a traitor to your family, Bianca. And no daughter of mine."

She tries to spit at me but can't quite make it work. The spittle simply dribbles down the side of her face. I lean in and wipe it off with the blade of the knife.

Her gaze has become unhinged, as if she knows it's the end of the road for her, and she's losing what little grip on reality she had. The whites are showing all around her dark irises, and her mouth is clamped into a thin line. Her eyes dart from side to side, calculating. Watching for her chance to kill us all.

"Won't let you...get...away..." I fall to one side, suddenly unable to tell which way is up, and land in a strong pair of arms that grab me and hold me firm.

"Rio." I look up at him, blinking when his face drifts in and out of focus. "And the goons." There seem to be hundreds of them here, crowding in behind Rio. "Always the goons. Too late today. Too late. Gentlemen…meet my momma…"

I start laughing again when my words distort and then moan as the pain in my arm grows to an unbearable level.

"Hurts," I whimper, and Rio's arms tighten slightly around me.

"We're getting you help, little bird. Doctor is on his way. Hold on, my darling. Stay strong."

My mother starts to laugh, sounding just like me. We are peas in a pod, her and me. Except I'm not like her. I don't want to be like her in any way.

"So touching," she sneers. "The Agosti love birds, carousing in all the blood and gore."

"Give me the knife, Bianca," Rio says softly in my ear.

He tries to take it from my clenched fist, but I pull back, not letting him.

"Uh-uh. Gotta kill her. Gotta get rid of this monster, Rio. Before she gets rid of us."

"I know, my love. We will. *I* will. I'll do it for you. For my parents. For Francine. For all of our dead and injured."

I shake my head again, trying to fight against the encroaching darkness. "*My* momma. *My* mess. Gotta…"

"Bianca." This time when Rio reaches for the knife, I have no strength left in my fingers to stop him. "If I let you kill this woman, my darling, it will rip your soul in two. Let me do it for you. Because I love you."

I blink again, certain my vision has disintegrated. Because it looks like Rio has tears in his eyes, and my husband never cries. Except in the pool that one time. And I made sure no one else saw that. Unless my memory is playing tricks on me while my body falls apart.

Because I really don't feel very good at all…

"We do it…" I focus and finally manage to get the word out of my mouth. "Together."

Love and sympathy shine from Rio's eyes, and he nods gently, then holds out the knife.

I lay my good hand over his but then tighten my fingers, hesitating. This is my mother. I'm about to cross a bridge to a place I can never come back from. Doubt fills me, and I lift my hand from his.

"Maybe not… I don't think I can…"

"It's all right, darling. I've got you."

"I curse you, Bianca Agosti." My mother hurls the sudden words up into my face. "And I curse your husband and everyone you love. And most of all, I curse your daughter, Em—"

Rio's hand plunges down with the knife, straight into Rina's throat, stopping her from finishing our daughter's name out loud. She dies instantly, the crazy light leaving her eyes, with only a single gurgle and a small spurt of blood spilling up and out of her mouth.

I stare down at the knife with Rio clutching the handle. And my hand grasping Rio's. When did I place my hand back on his?

I don't care. She's gone. And we're safe.

Our enemy has been slain, and we did it together. And in doing so, we gave our family one more chance to live another day.

The darkness takes me then, and as I fall into oblivion, I wonder if I now have an inner monster just like Rio's.

26

"Hate never can win a heart, only love can do that."
Debasish Mridha

Rio

I CAN BARELY STAND to let Bianca out of my sight. She almost died from the loss of blood, and the pain in my heart when I thought I was going to lose her...

Our field doctor did his best, as he always does for us, but in the end, he wasn't able to do what he needed to at our home, and she had to be airlifted to the Agosti organization's private hospital north of Boston.

It was sheer luck that the helicopter and pilot were still on the premises, thanks to Carnarvon, so in a strange way, he and Rina saved Bianca's life. She spent three days in the hospital's intensive care unit, with me by her side, before being transferred to a general room—where she was delighted to discover her bodyguard Lee still recuperating only two doors up from her own room.

I would be jealous of their budding friendship if I wasn't so certain that Bianca loves me as much as I love her. And, of course, the fact that Leon is more likely to date one of my male bodyguards than a woman. That helps to curb my jealousy. A little.

She clings to me all the time as if I am her support person. It makes me want to be better, and bigger, and stronger, simply because she needs it. I want to be her everything, the way she has become mine.

Now that she's home, back at the house here in Brookline that we've decided to make our main residence, I find myself trailing around after her like a lovesick puppy. Pathetic, of course. But I won't have it any other way.

She is my sun, moon, and stars, all rolled into one, as the books and movies say.

I never believed in love, not completely, until I almost lost her.

While she was still in the hospital, and drifting in and out of consciousness, I promised Bianca I would arrange to relocate the animal shelter we were building at the riverside to the adjacent property here in Brookline.

My new lawyer, Dana's uncle, has already commenced the paperwork to purchase the land from the current owners next door, as well as obtain the necessary permits. Bianca will have plenty to keep her occupied in the future. When she's well enough.

Right now, tucked up in our bed with her hair falling down over her shoulders, no makeup on, and her freckles shining across her nose, I have never loved nor desired her more. But I am trying to tamp down my desire because she needs rest more than she needs my greedy cock.

"Are you going to join me tonight?" She sounds frustrated, and I frown at her petulant tone.

I *have* been sleeping with her, but on top of the covers so we can be close and I can hold her in my arms, but I won't be tempted to touch her in an intimate way.

"You are still recovering, Bianca…"

"Rio. I *am* recovered. I am whole, and I am well, at least physically. Mentally… Well, you know. That'll take a while, but I'm seeing that counsellor they set me up with at the hospital next week." She sighs loudly. "Honestly, if you don't get into this bed and make love with me tonight, I'll… I'll…"

"You'll what, little bird?"

"I'll order a sex toy online, and then I'll never need you again."

That is not what I expected her to say.

"Well." I slide off the boxers I was going to wear to bed then lift the covers and slip beneath them with her, naked together for the first time in a while. "You are always very welcome to purchase a sex toy, but you won't be allowed to use it unless I am there to direct its use."

She shimmies across and wraps her arms and legs around me, clinging like a limpet. Her skin against mine is warm, and there's a clean scent wafting from her hair that tickles my nostrils and calms me.

Bianca smells like home.

"I don't want rough, or quick, or dirty tonight," she says. "I just want you, Rio. Gentle. Please?"

I roll us to the side so we're facing each other and then slip my fingers into her hair to cradle the back of her head. I draw her close and claim her mouth in a slow, delicious kiss.

"Like that?" I ask when I release her lips.

I kiss her again then rock against her hip, keeping my movement gentle even though my cock is already hard just from being in proximity to her beautiful heat. My gut flip-flops when she presses her pelvis back against me, pushing her mound into the top of my leg and grinding gently.

"Oh, yes," she sighs, and we rock gently back and forth against each other as pleasure ripples through me. "Just like that."

The build of desire is slow and steady, the heat and heaviness between my legs no less intense than it always is with Bianca. In fact, the depth of my need seems greater this time, the fire spreading through my veins to encompass every cell in my body. I revel in the feel of her fingertips exploring my back as I begin to stroke and explore her curves in return.

"I thought I'd lost you, *mia cara*," I murmur, pressing kisses to her now-closed eyes, the edges of her mouth, and then down the line of her neck to her breast.

I lift a hand and caress her nipple before tweaking it between my thumb and forefinger. She shudders beneath me and releases a groan, her pussy leaving a trail of wetness across my hip and groin as she shifts a little to line us up more exactly.

"You will never lose me," she says, lifting one of her legs higher around my waist and opening her pussy wide. Ready for me. "I love you, Rio."

"And I love you, little bird. You own my heart."

I adjust my hips and push the head of my cock inside her, the entry effortless and perfect.

She moans and bears down, encouraging every inch of me to find its way home. "You own my heart and my body. I am yours, Rio. Always."

When I begin to move, thrusting back and forth inside her, she releases another tiny moan that tears at my insides and loosens my control.

"I feel you," she cries, "deep inside me. Right at my core, Rio. Oh, yes, that's perfect... Please don't stop..."

The clenching of her pussy around my cock is the signal for me to fully let go, and as she begins to shudder in my arms and cry out her release, I join her in climax, growling deep in my throat as the rush of heat and heaviness bursts free from my cock and my orgasm shatters me into pieces.

Later, much later, when we come back to earth, I kiss her bare shoulder and give her a little nip there. "Next time, my beautiful wife, please do not remove the knife from any wound. That will help to contain the bleeding."

She shakes with sudden laughter. "Next time? Please, God, let it be some time before there's a next time. If at all." She stops laughing and comes up onto her elbow, looking down at my face with a suddenly serious expression. "Rio, there's something I need to tell you."

"Oh?" I smooth my thumb over her lips, enjoying their lush plumpness and the slightly darker pink color that always seems to happen after our lovemaking. "What is it, Bianca?"

She smiles shyly then takes one of my hands and brings it down to cup her abdomen. "I hope you're ready for this."

I lift the bedcovers and stare down at her gently curving stomach. "Are you... Are we..."

She nods, and it is as if the sun has just broken through the clouds on a stormy day.

As the realization dawns about what she's telling me, the darkness in my world recedes just that little bit more. For the first time in what feels like forever, there is genuine hope in my heart for the joy that tomorrow might bring.

I hope you enjoyed the *Dark Enemies* trilogy. If so, please consider leaving a review.

Keep an eye out for *Reckless Heir*, Nikolas's and Daniela's story—book one in the *Dark Vows* duet.

Sign up for Zoe Delaney's reader newsletter at her website and never miss a new release:

www.Zoe-Delaney.com

ABOUT THE AUTHOR

Zoe Delaney is the dark contemporary romantic suspense pen name of *USA Today* bestselling author, Jen Katemi.

When Zoe isn't writing, she runs an editing and proofreading business, dotes on her daughters and pampers various cats—including a rescue with one hip. She lives in Melbourne, Australia.

Find out more or sign up for her reader newsletter at her website and never miss a new release:

www.Zoe-Delaney.com

BOOKS BY ZOE DELANEY

Dark Enemies series
Ruthless Possession
Ruthless Betrayal
Ruthless Enemy

Dark Vows series
Reckless Heir
Reckless King

Made in United States
Orlando, FL
02 May 2025

60986402R00120